I0651427

Francis Walker

Letters of a Baritone

Francis Walker

Letters of a Baritone

ISBN/EAN: 9783744716567

Printed in Europe, USA, Canada, Australia, Japan

Cover: Foto ©Andreas Hilbeck / pixelio.de

More available books at **www.hansebooks.com**

Letters of a Baritone

by
Francis Walker

London
William Heinemann
1895

To My Sister

A noble woman and a true artist

THE HOUSE.

There is no architect
    Can build as the Muse can;
She is skilful to select
    Materials for her plan.

.   .   .   .

She lays her beams in music,
    In music every one,
To the cadence of the whirling world
    Which dances round the sun;

That so they shall not be displaced
    By lapses or by wars,
But, for the love of happy souls,
    Outlive the newest stars.

EMERSON.

CONTENTS

Contents

Contents

ix

b

Contents

INTRODUCTORY LETTER

INTRODUCTORY LETTER

London, April, 1894.

MY DEAR SISTER:

The bulky packet of my old letters which you gave me last year—those sent you from Florence when I was studying singing in that charming city—now returns to you in this form. They are published with the sincere desire to make easier for others the way which for me was fraught with difficulties. Those difficulties were not merely the ordinary ones that beset the stranger in a strange land. Truly, they are always many for the student who, not overburdened with money, and therefore anxious to accomplish much in a short time, goes to a foreign country provided with but meagre instruction as to how he may live there safely and economically.

Before such a venture it is well to know what preparation to make for it, and especially how to avoid the pitfalls of charlatanism. The unscrupulous, plausible wrecker of voices is found everywhere, but the thoughtful student may learn how to avoid him at home and abroad—in fact he must learn many things from every other to whose thoughts he has access. *Experientia docet* is a maxim that holds forever good, but it is too often thought to mean that each must gain his experience for himself, and we forget, or refuse to avail ourselves of, the time-saving help others can give us.

It is my earnest hope that these letters, written to you to whom it has ever been a pleasure to relate freely all things which have befallen me as student and singer, may be of interest and use to many in our profession and to those desirous of entering it. To some they may afford help to clarify things and theories about which doubts have arisen. For others there is practical information about the cost of living and studying in Italy ; and perhaps some will find herein sympathy and encouragement, if they too work against great disadvantages and grow weary and despondent upon that long, steep path which must be travelled by whoever would arrive at any excellence in vocal art.

I have aimed to be fair in my description of Italy as a land toward which students of singing should continue to direct their steps. I am always grateful for what the song-dowered country has given to me, and the deep sense of my indebtedness to her has made it a pleasant task to send back thus to your keeping the letters which recount the experiences of my student-days in Florence. Written as they were to you—the choicest of comrades—they may be helpful to some who, like yourself, cannot turn from the nearer duties to travel afar. Such may, perhaps, by some things in these pages, be at least aroused to fresh enthusiasm for the greatness and beauty of the art of song.

You will remember that those old letters contained some things which might possibly have been allowed to keep place herein, had it been my design to make a book acceptable to the widest conceivable circle of readers. They have been cut out to make room for whatever was likely to be of more direct use to singers, to students of singing, and to lovers of music generally. Still, with the belief firmly fixed in my mind that every serious student needs to keep himself in touch with all the arts and with all beauty, I have ventured to retain in my pages some of the necessarily sketchy descriptions of things and scenes which were to me valuable or beautiful. Many such details, which at a first glance may seem extraneous to the main purpose of the book, will perhaps ultimately be found confluent with that purpose, and of interest as having belonged to the daily life of a student who was in great earnest to make all sources feed him in his growth into an artist.

A recent visit to Florence and more study there with the maestro to whom I owe the rescue and rehabilitation of my voice, make the opportunity for me to confirm now my estimate of Italy and Italian teaching as set forth in the following letters. Those brilliant days of late summer and early autumn ! Those rich hours in the cool, airy studio over the gardens of belated roses and spice-breathing oleanders ! How full of gain was all the time ! Blessed with abundant strength, the things that seemed only far-off possibilities in the old days were attained almost at a bound.

Florence was very beautiful to me, and all

the Tuscan country about had even more than the old charm in its highways and by-ways. Never before had the towers of the lovely city seemed to spring so lightly into air so delicately azure, and never before had the valleys and hills beyond her battlemented walls been so alluring. Around all lay Italy—bright Italy, which has given me so much that now I cannot do less than try in this poor fashion to win for her the affection and interest of those who should surely love her for the sake of the art she has ever cherished with true devotion.

LETTER I.

LETTER I

A Dream set to Music.—In Italy to Study Singing.—
A Refreshing Voyage and a Rested Voice.—First
Night at the Opera.—Italian and American Theatres Compared.—Florence.—A Student's Hopes
and Aspirations.—No " Royal Road."—" *Chi va
piano va sano.*"

Florence, December 30, 188–.

D O you know that strange experience of
seeming, just between sleeping and
waking, to float as a sort of spirit in
a void, and gradually to acquire perception
and sensation ?   It has come to me sometimes,
and it was in that curious half-world I groped
about, two days since, on the morning of
December 28th, for what seemed a long time,
but was probably the merest moment, so
delicately are one's faculties poised in that
misty instant, so capable of far and easy
flight in search of the path which leads back

from the world of dreams to that of realities. I had slept but two or three hours, and in a light calm, my first peaceful slumber for many days. There came up toward me, filling what had been emptiness, a rich tide of music which I presently recognized as the sound of singing voices helped by the dramatic colour of strings; but before I could think of it all as music the words of a soft, strange tongue shaped themselves to my ear, and with a slow, vague, ever-increasing content, I knew I was in Italy! Still the moment of waking was delayed, and my dream-self went back over all the blue and green of Mediterranean and Atlantic. Again I felt the rolling of the ship, heard the wash of waves and the musical yo-ho-ing of the sailors as they tugged at the canvases. Again I heard the howling of the great storm the far side of Portugal, and the shrieks of the even grander one this side of Spain. Again uprose upon the night that crescent of twinkling lights, growing steadily to a wide, glittering amphitheatre which meant—Genoa! All the while—what brief while it may have been—the mingled sounds of voices and sweet wild tones of guitars and mandolines

came nearer, and brought me more and more
clearly the words :

> " *Rondinella pellegrina*
> *Che ti pose sul verone,*
> *Ricantando ogni mattina*
> *Quella flebile canzone ;*
> *Che vuoi dirmi in tua favella,*
> *Pellegrina rondinella ?* "

It all grew to such wide, rich reverbera-
tion that I finally became conscious that the
musicians—perhaps some band of workmen
going forth in the early morning — were
coming up through the Galleria Mazzini,
close under the windows of my room in the
Hôtel Isotta, and that I was, for the night and
the day, a dweller in Genoa, " *La Superba.*"
Far as that of the " pilgrim swallow " in the
chorus swelling so splendidly through the
stillness of dawn, had been my journey
" from lands of snow to lands of sun."

From prairies wind-swept and snow-man-
tled to this Italy, drenched in warm sunshine ! and certainly no singer could have
more perfect rest for his worn nerves and
tired throat than this voyage of seventeen
days from New York had given me. For
two weeks not a note did I sing, and on

Christmas-eve, off the coast of Valencia, at the end of a most perfect blue day—a blue that was all one tint in sky and sea—I sang some simple ballads, little, tender, homely things, and found the voice rested and resonant. I decided upon this rather unusual route because of the complete and long repose it would give me, as well as because of its cheapness.

But it was so long and monotonous that every step of my wandering about that quaint Genoa was a delight. And how refreshing was the drive far up the hill-streets, near some of the many fortresses, past gardens so cunningly sloped toward the sun that they were well-nigh as colourful as our gardens are in early autumn. Dark cypresses pressed sombre, cushiony boughs against the high, gray stone walls; there was green grass upon the up-slanting lawns, and thereon burned vividly masses of scarlet geraniums and salvias. After the voyage over all those leagues of deep monotones of colour, it was most truly "the splendour of the grass and the glory of the flower."

Can you imagine what joy it was to find a fairly good opera company performing in

Genoa, so that I could hear grand opera my very first night in Italy? For one franc I had an excellent seat in the parquette of the Teatro Politeama and settled myself comfortably there to hear "L'Africaine."

How different from our opera-houses was the theatre! At first it seemed bare and poor, but soon I began to realize how we, with our ever-increasing passion for luxury and show, offer up Art as a sacrifice upon the altar of that unworthy appetite. We must have all the floors of our theatres richly carpeted, and then covered again by rows of upholstered chairs, so that the whole area is one great cushion ready to absorb and smother sound. Heavy draperies must be hung in every possible place—before the stage, in the boxes, and at every doorway—and so far from being satisfied with that, we must, forsooth! carry rich festoons of velvet or satin over the fronts of galleries and boxes. And the inevitable consequence is that not for one instant in a long evening's work, is any singer heard with that ultimate, far-reaching brilliancy of *timbre* which convinces the ear and captivates the soul. The fine quality of individuality, which for lack of a better term we call " magnetism," is quite lost.

The fact is that we keep our singers working under hopeless conditions, struggling against an arbitrary material environment which stifles at its birth much artistic effort. Padding and cushions everywhere, instead of clear space and firm surfaces to develop and reflect sound and inspire the singer. Everything to hinder and nothing to help. The voice, to be at its best, needs space in which to travel forth and exult in freedom, else the soul of the singer cannot expand, feed upon itself, and create an empyrean in which it can fuse into one the voice and itself. I am told that all Italian theatres have to Americans the meagre look of which I spoke, and that fact affords me some new lights.

We often speak of the futility of possessing voice without soul to guide it and to be its needed complement, in order to secure lofty expression in song ; and this first experience in Italian theatres has suggested to me another and even subtler dualism of force. I have, for the first time in my operatic experience, either as artist or listener only, felt an audi-

ence taking its proper share in the rendering
of an opera. These people who listened to
Meyerbeer's somewhat insincere music, heard
it given by a tolerable orchestra, a very inefficient chorus, and artists of but mediocre
ability. They chatted with most amiable
unconcern all through the first scene. That
over, I could distinctly feel myself swept on
toward an approaching hush of expectation
—a something coming ! Over and over
again in the course of the opera, the tide of
careless, murmuring talk arose—never when
any solo work was being done, but during
the familiar ensemble portions which did
not enchain the general interest. Then it
was followed by the premonitory hush, and
each time that silence led the way to some
brilliant point of the opera which everybody seemed on the alert to expect and
enjoy.

When it arrived, those directly employed
in its execution, whether orchestra, chorus,
or soloists, or all together, had the straightforward sympathy and the tangible, though
subtle, help of the entire audience. I could
not but give it favourable contrast with our
calm, collected, coldly critical publics and

their leaning - back, lapped - in - luxury, "please-amuse-me" sort of manner. And the difference in the auditoriums seems to me largely responsible for the difference in the musical results. With the house such as gives the voice, or instrument, free play, the artist has "great moments"—is upheld—grips the listener, who answers quickly to the touch, exactly as an "echo-organ" is played at a distance from the main one by the player who knows how cunningly the electric connection has made it possible for him to compel it to call back its clear, sweet, answering, helping accords.

Well, I can only sum it up briefly by saying that I learned that night how the dual forces—audience and performers—may be drawn by each other into a strong tide of interwoven cause and effect, yielding a certain intenser form of art-pleasure than I have hitherto experienced in operatic annals.

Yesterday morning, December 29th, I took the train at Genoa and arrived here at nine o'clock last night. To-day, after reading the huge packet of welcome home-letters, my first task is to send you this to tell you of my arrival and my plans. Many have come to Italy to study singing better equipped with voice and health, but I have abundance of hope and courage. Nor is a certain large faith lacking. I have not "hitched my wagon to a star," but to a whole constellation, for if one thing in the realm of musical art is not attainable, another may be, and the only matter which presently concerns me is to take the step on which the light falls, and to believe the next will be likewise illuminated in good time.

I shall study just as if Italian opera were my goal, because that is the only career in Italy for the singer. Such study must be, with a process of assimilation coming after it, a good preparation for other lines of work, and I fully realize that the greater part of the teaching I have hitherto had, was so faulty, and has left such bad effects upon my voice, that it is impossible now to know what that voice is really worth, and what work it will ultimately be fit to do. I shall, without any serious concern for the future, walk in the path now before me. I shall learn to sing as well as possible, and perhaps the day will come when there will be no need to confine my work to the rather empty forms of the conventional Italian répertoire, which, as a phase of study, is certainly valuable enough.

My prime need is, as you know, a thorough "placing" of the voice. Can the teacher be found to help me on so far? What failures in the cases of his predecessors in office might be put on record! One such, in particular, is scarcely to be regretted, inasmuch as it brought me, first, acquaintance, then lasting friendship, with one of the most fascinating and brilliant of men, and a conscientious, untiring worker. That he could not make a success with my voice should probably be largely laid to the previous bad work done, which had misplaced it, obscured whatever good qualities it inherently possessed, and so made it very difficult to understand and to treat. He at least imparted to me something of musical taste and style, insisted by precept and example upon my becoming as sound a musical scholar as possible, and fostered in me the conviction that an unswerving purpose, united with earnestness, industry, and lofty ideals, would open the way to a career of usefulness in some field.

But he was thoroughly imbued with the

American spirit of unrest, and could not
work with sufficient simplicity of method.
It is a national characteristic, and militates
strongly against any sound artistic progress.
The inventive faculty is too often misused.
In the education of a musical artist there is
small place for it, so subtle is the process,
and so much time must be allowed at each
of its stages for the ripening of newly developed powers. The shoal of self-styled
"Voice Builders" in our country do an in-
calculable mischief to art. The people who
talk and write volubly of their theories and
experiments, and who invent machines to
teach singing with, are, more or less consciously, humbugs. There is no royal road
for the student of singing—no "short cut"
—and the sooner we realize that the older
methods are still the best, the sooner we
shall begin to form true artists.

The ancient Egyptians enveloped their
mummies in finer linen than our best looms
can produce to-day. Modern processes have
but increased the quantity of the fabric.
Likewise there are more singers in the latter
half of this century than existed in its first
half, but if we could show the world another

Pasta she might have had, like her great predecessor, to study seven years to acquire a perfect trill. There is too much haste. We have industry—because ambition is always at its back to bolster it up—but we lack patience. Louis Ehlert, who has put many things into happiest expression in his "Letters on Music," says: "Bound down to tradition, originality is forced to win freedom through slow cultivation, as a young tree is at first supported, that it may grow uprightly and avoid deformity. The artist who misses or arrogantly breaks away from this natural process of development, will be punished by his own roughness and want of taste. . . . his share in the history of art will be denied."

My time here in Italy must, alas! be brief—two years at the utmost—but those two years will represent neither the beginning nor end of study. They must at least be made to give material for future use. As you know, I came with the express purpose of obtaining the tuition of the famous *maestro di canto*, Sig. O——, so now must leave this and set about the business of getting settled in rooms where lessons can be commenced without delay.

LETTER II

LETTER II

Florence, January, 188–.

NEEDING, first of all things, some information about rooms, prices, etc.,
I called at once upon the American
consul, who was most friendly and obliging.
Declaring that he knew the very man who
could best help me to what was required,
and who himself was a student of singing,
he wrote me a line of introduction—which
I immediately started to deliver — to Mr.
George T——. He was at home in his
pretty apartment in the Piazza Carraia, and
was just singing the last phrase of the " *Salve,
dimora,*" when the pretty, dark-eyed *came-
riera* opened the door for me. He received
me cordially, and after dismissing his accom-

panist, went forth with me to look for rooms. His fluent Italian cleared away all difficulties, and we soon found and engaged a large sitting-room and bed-room adjoining. They are in the Borg' Ognissanti, a quaint, busy street which lies just back of the Arno and extends from the Carraia bridge westward toward the Cascine. Great, gaunt, cavernous rooms they are, but well furnished in rather ugly modern Italian fashion, with the regulation tables, sofas, and chairs set in stiff order upon the floors of shining Venetian mosaic. The ceilings are high and deeply vaulted, and as little of the winter sunshine enters my south windows because of the lofty buildings opposite, it is not always easy to keep comfortably warm.

My rent is fifty francs a month, and my *padrone*, a professional cook, furnishes my modest meals at a charge which I have already discovered to be quite high, although it would seem almost absurdly cheap in an American city. I have also found that the mistakes of foreigners here lie chiefly in paying foreigners' prices, and in not taking into account that, while the main items of living expenses are comparatively small, every little extra supply and service must be paid for, so that it is difficult to keep the total down to a reasonable figure. By foreigners' prices I mean that all things to be bought or hired are bargained for, and as soon as a *forestiere* is recognized, most dealers ask him a price about double that which an Italian would give. But it is always done good-naturedly, and if one takes a little trouble to learn the just values of things, the amiable haggling over prices is taken as a matter of course by both dealer and buyer. Mr. T—— thinks my living a marvel of cheapness, but I must do still better, and am convinced that a way to do so will open, though some mistakes will doubtless be made at first in trying to follow it.

As soon as I was comfortably settled and had a small, but tolerable, piano hired for fifteen francs a months, I made inquiries about the celebrated *maestro di canto*, Signor O——, with the intention of beginning lessons at soon as he would receive me. Mr. T—— had studied with him, but, for some reason that I could not at first discover, had discontinued his lessons. He spoke with some reserve about it, but said warmly enough that Signor O—— was a great master of vocal style and just the man with whom to get up an operatic répertoire. Of course I know my need to be anything but a répertoire just yet—time enough for that when the voice is " placed "—but his reputation is great and he has well-known artists among his former pupils, and besides, as Mr. T—— justly remarked, I would not, after the long journey taken for the purpose, be satisfied without trying his teaching. Therefore it seemed best to seek him and engage lessons, for which he charges ten francs an hour to students destined for the musical profession. Provided with the letters of introduction given to me by several of his American pupils, I went to his house and found him at home, but had to wait some time for him to finish a lesson then in progress.

When he entered the room to greet me, which he did with much cordiality, I found him to be a bland, courteous, elderly man, of medium height, rather stoutly built, and having a florid, good-humored face. He talked a little of his old pupils who had given me the letters, and seemed much interested in hearing of their success as singers

and teachers, and then he readily promised
to give me lessons, not even finding it necessary to hear my voice before consenting
to teach me. I had always supposed it
difficult to get lessons, from him. This did
not seem like it, but perhaps my introduc-
tions cleared away some ordinary obstacles,
and made him so willing to receive me as a
student. The price is, as I have told you,
ten francs an hour for professional pupils,
and that is the largest fee paid by such students in all Italy. One detail of the arrangement surprised me much; he preferred
coming to my rooms for the lessons, saying it
gave him needed exercise to attend most of
his students at their homes.

On the following Tuesday he drove up to
my door in his little carriage, and after a
fatherly sort of greeting he ran his handsome, facile hands over the keys of the
piano, selected "*In questa tomba*" from my
music, and desired me to sing it. I felt terribly nervous, knowing my voice to be in a
chaotic condition, and being far from strong
enough to cope well with those long, swelling phrases. But of course I went through
the song, and with what seemed to me small

help from his accompaniment, which lacked
the organ-like fulness and breadth Beethoven
must surely have intended in the simple but
massive harmonies. Particularly did I miss
the steady, sonorous *crescendo* needed in the
chords played *tremolando* under the line :

e   non,   e   non bag-nar mie

ce - ne - ri d'in - u - ti - le   ve - len.

I knew the song in a manner, by heart,
but had never studied it so as to know accu-
rately its rhythmical values, so sang out of
time in several places, which fault the maestro duly pointed out to me. One must always make allowance for the expansive kindness of temperament and not take an Italian's
praises too literally, so there was no occasion
for much vanity when Signor O——— said
I sang well. He added that my need was
more variety of tone-color. In singing he
would not, he said, advise me to open the
mouth as widely as has been my habit.
After I had sung some scales and *arpeggi*, he

said he would bring me some *solfeggi* for the next lesson, and then he wanted more songs, choosing first "*Il balen*," from "Trovatore." He approved the phrasing I had learned, but stopped me at times to get certain modulations of tone. Once my voice broke slightly upon the vowel *e*, and he immediately set to work to show me how to place the tone more securely by smiling a little, in order to direct the sound farther forward.

After that I sang the entire scena from Verdi's "Nabuco." Do you remember it? The recitative begins, "*Sperate, O figli!*" The andante which follows it is one of great breadth and beauty, but the cabaletta, "*Come notte a sol fulgente*," is quite trivial. I had studied it all with Madame K——, who of all my teachers did me the most good. In it he was satisfied with the phrasing and style, but found the voice forced in the highest notes of the andante, and totally unequal to the lowest ones. In both extremes it was lacking in solidity and security.

For my next lesson Signor O—— will bring me, he says, besides the promised *sol-*

feggi, '' one leetle Italian song.'' I wish he
would not, but could not say that it seemed
to me vitally necessary to keep to more technical work to place the voice so that it can
be used with freedom and certainty. None
know better than ourselves that a first lesson
is, for both teacher and pupil, insufficient
ground upon which to base a final opinion,
and I hope Signor O——— does not from
this one form a judgment of my abilities any
more than I do of his. By the latter phrase
I do not mean that it is for me to doubt his
great and proven ability, but all teachers
make their failures as well as their successes,
and it is possible that he has gone away convinced that I have not sufficient voice or
talent ever to do him credit, and so will not
trouble himself to teach me with the exacting thoroughness so much needed. At any
rate, it is now my business to follow closely
in my study all his suggestions and directions, and so prove to him that I am at least
diligent and in great earnest.

Buying supplies in the shops and markets
is an amusing diversion. My *padrone* furnishes me neither wine, fruit, fuel, nor lights,
so I go every morning to the Mercato Vec-

chio (Old Market), among all the little stalls set duskily, like small caves, into or against the walls of the ancient houses. They glow with the hundred hues of flowers or with the warm tints of the piled-up nuts and fruits. I descend into a grimy cellar and order baskets of pine-cones and wood. Candles are perhaps to be bought, and there are shops exclusively for them. One that I know is an odd sight. The front of it, filled with ranks and rows of candles of all sizes, from a tiny taper up to a huge, painted altar-candle, looks at a distance like an organ with its pipes of varying lengths and sizes.

For wine, which I do not like and only drink because it is said to be necessary to health, I bought a *fiasco*—a big, bulbous bottle covered with a rough basket-work made of reeds or straw, and containing about two and a half quarts of red wine which seems pure, but is crude and rough to the taste. This quantity costs me one franc sixty centimes — about thirty - two cents. Fruits, fresh and dried, are also cheap and varied. Fuel is a far more serious item of expense in my *ménage*. It is never cheap in

Florence, amd this January weather, though bright and lovely, is very cold for the climate, so one is compelled, for safety's sake, to have good fires. It is said that a stranger feels keenly the cold of a first winter in Florence. Sunny rooms are a necessity here, and I must find such for myself.

January 6th. — To-day Signor O—— came a little later than the hour appointed for my second lesson, and was profuse in his apologies. It certainly did not matter, because I cannot sing anything like an hour— the voice not being posed so as to endure so much work at a stretch. We went over some scale-forms and he said I had evidently practised them well, but cautioned me not to fatigue the throat with them. Next we read some of the Concone Studies for baritone, which I have long known and used. After he had indicated in them various small matters of phrasing we turned from them to the "leetle Italian song" he had brought. It proved to be "*L'Eremitá*," ("*The Hermit*"), a fairly picturesque and musicianly trifle by Mililotti, in which a well-

written accompaniment comes to the rescue
of a meagre melody.

For making "points" in a song Signor
O——'s excellence is at once notable. He
understands exactly what the composer
means, and as exactly when to amplify those
hinted intentions so as to make all possible
effect with the composition. I begin to
comprehend why he is so highly approved
as a maestro with whom to study operas.
Whatever his gifts may be as a trainer of
voices, his tact and experience, his subtle
musical feeling, and his knowledge of traditions must enable him to fit each phrase of
a rôle to the singer's capacity.

I regret to learn that your throat is not
yet well and strong—that it still shows the
"granulation" which has been there ever
since your voice was a little strained ; but I
have repeatedly known such results to follow
like experiences, and am certain that this
trouble is not irremediable. We often hear
the throat spoken of as a delicate structure,
while in fact perhaps no part of the human
organism is so forgiving and possessed of
such wonderful powers of recuperation. Do
you remember how this weakness first showed

itself in the scraping sound which accompanied the tones about the F , and how it came as a direct con- sequence of "opening" the voice up to that point?

Since your experience I have met several sopranos with much the same trouble in that vocal region, always the result of bad training. The mischief was generally perpetrated by some self-styled "voice-builder." The very term is misleading, because building is done from below upward, and that is exactly what is wrong in making a voice. The majority of untrained voices which are high enough to go to the tones above that F show some weakness thereabouts, and the common mistake is to attempt to strengthen that weak and uncertain spot from below by using the so-called "opening" process. It means crowding on muscular force in the upward scale, necessarily bearing hard upon the throat and so getting the voice, in the region indicated, very broad, coarse, and totally incapable of modulation. The quick access of power by such treatment is sometimes startling. Too often the student is flattered by it and expects to get similar development of the entire compass, and then afterward acquire smoothness.

Never was there a greater mistake — a more fallacious manner of vocal education. It is all wrong end first and can only result in an uneven scale and an unmanageable voice, with tones of abnormal strength in one or two spots — a voice which drifts farther and farther away from all chance of doing artistic singing. The process, from the very beginning, should be exactly reversed, and the strengthening of the weaker tones effected by working from above downward.

Roughly speaking, the tones of an untrained soprano have, up to a certain quality, while a quite different texture characterizes those above —leaving the space between the *C* and the *F* a sort of doubtful ground ; and it is there that nine-tenths of the battles between right and wrong in voice training are fought for the weal or woe of the singer. The difficulties in that region for the soprano and mezzo-soprano find almost an exact parallel in the tenor and baritone voices. In all voices wherein that uncertain spot is found the quality of tone above it should be gradually and carefully brought downward, generally as far as ♪ thus lapping the higher register down over the lower.

There are then two available qualities of tone, one delicate and pure, growing stronger by use, and ultimately capable of swelling with firmness and grandeur into the other and broader tone. In such treatment lies the only salvation for voices naturally of uneven scale, or those made uneven by false teaching.

I am already finding opportunities of observation here, and shall write you again about this particular matter. The great trouble in putting such things on paper is, of course, the difference in the terms by which different people allude to the same things, but you and I have worked together enough to understand each other, so that although I might not be able to put these hints into a book or a newspaper article with any hope of helping many readers, they can perhaps be formulated so as to be of use to you. How heedlessly teachers and writers quarrel over their different systems of nomenclature.

It is the greatest mistake not to know and use all the varying names and phrases for the subtleties involved in the teaching of singing. The teacher who allows himself but one unvarying formula of expression must fail to reach about three-fourths of the intelligences represented in his pupils. It suggests the bed of Procrustes, does it not?

January 10th. — Another lesson to - day. First some scales and then the Concone Studies. After those a new song called "*Non cambia mai*," by Mariani. The maestro filled it full of charming " points " for me, suggesting with his pencil a *mezzo-sospiro* here, a delicate *portamento* there, a brilliant attack in one place, a sudden change of quality in another—all those things which simulate emotion in the singing, and sometimes even create it in the singer as he does them. He praised my work and found the voice more firm and equal. But these little songs elude me so provokingly. At times they go well, and then again I cannot sing them at all. They are too high—not because the highest notes and phrases are out of my vocal range, but because I have no settled method of production there. Scarcely ten words has he as yet given me about that, but he may be coming to it duly. *Pazienza !*

Am I as happy as I expected to be here in Italy, you ask. Yes, it is a new and fas-cinating world all about me, though of course study is the greatest joy. Though never content, I am always happy ; why not? Over ninety-nine hundredths of the people I know I have the priceless advantage of loving my work.

LETTER III

LETTER III

Florence, February, 188–.
Ash Wednesday.

I WRITE you from a sunny apartment of three tiny rooms in the Piazza Carraia.

Until this place was vacated and made ready for me, I shivered in my caves in the Borg' Ognissanti, and finally brought away from there a severe cold which caused some interruption in my study. In making the move I took the opportunity of also changing my small piano for a huge Neumayer which is most inspiring in the volume and duration of its tone. I treated my cold with an inha-

43

lation of *catrame*—tar-water—atomized by a jet of steam from a little boiler set over a spirit-lamp. It is a favorite remedy here with singers, and succeeded admirably in my case by reaching and healing the affected tissues.

Upon resuming lessons, Signor O—— declared my voice was smoother for the period of repose, and began at once to give me some operatic work. Granted that I am fit to begin such study, I think his selections entirely judicious. The first one was the pretty cantabile, " *O, divina Agnese !* " from Bellini's "Beatrice di Tenda," and then followed the well-known air, " *Eri tu,*" from Verdi's " Ballo in Maschera." But since accumulating a little répertoire of these things and the songs which preceded them, the lesson-hour is taken up with them to the exclusion of scales and *solfeggi*. I work at them as well as I can, but one needs outside criticism in the matter of voice-placing. The maestro does not seem to take pleasure in doing that which is most needed—that which must be done before I can do any satisfactory work with songs and operatic arias.

However, as long as he is my teacher, it is for me to work exactly as I am directed, affording him every chance of carrying out any intentions he may have. At present my questionings are to you and to myself; if I become convinced that he is not doing what is best for me, of course it will then be time to leave him. I trust it may not come to that, because I already feel attached to him, and his ability is so well attested in the artists he has everywhere before the public. Sometimes I doubt whether his natural charm of manner does not make me believe his interest in me is genuine.

Of late I have attended the opera often. There is a company at the Teatro Pagliano which contains some excellent artists, and so good are the chorus and orchestra that the ensemble is really strong. To me, the greatest novelty of the season is Gomez's opera, "Il Guarany," which was put on last week. Mr. T—— went with me to the cheap seats—very good ones in the rear rows of the parquette, but not so far back as to be under the balcony—one franc each. Presently the manager, whom Mr. T—— knows, came to us and insisted upon our accepting a vacant loggia in the first tier, and there he called upon us later in the evening. The opera is full of brilliant things, not always original, but impassioned and richly colored. The instrumentation is excellent, much fuller than in the works of the Donizetti-Bellini period, yet with no attempt at following the later German leadings. The story is South American, which affords the chance for much music in the fascinating Spanish rhythms. The most successful number of the kind is the brindisi for the baritone, in which the orchestra is, for the most part, audaciously turned into an enormous guitar, making a most exciting effect. The artist who had the part gave the song with tremendous spirit and had to repeat it. It is certainly the finest drinking song for baritone that I know in any opera.

All this reminds me of your coming musical event, the C—— Opera Festival, and you are to have Mme. X—— there. Be sure to hear her, but pray beforehand that the capricious woman may give you some of her really great moments. Go, if possible, when she sings in " Les Huguenots." She will make her entrance down the great staircase in the side of the scene, perhaps bowing and smiling to friends in the nearest boxes! She will sing well, with no great fervour, yet without giving you the feeling that she is economizing her powers. You will wonder if that is really the artist of whose ability as actress and singer you have heard so much, and your impatience will increase until you will wish almost anyone else had the part of Valentine.

Then, just as your disappointment over the many wasted opportunities reaches its climax, will come the grand duett of the fourth act. Little quivering chills will creep down your spine as you see the effect the music begins to have upon that curious creature. Upon her high cheek-bones the color concentrates and burns ; the eyes that have been too dreamy begin to dilate, and they fascinate you with the growing tragedy contained in their blue depths. They are eyes which despair, entreat, command, and which almost hold Raoul from his sworn duty. The woman is roused more and more with each recurrence of the phrase of the duett, mounting up to the *C-flat*—she towers as she sings it forth with splendid power—she·

crouches and staggers and half speaks, half sings her exclamations of horror—and then, as Raoul rushes from her to perish in the massacre outside, she falls to the floor just as you were feeling that you could scarcely bear another note of that maddening music, nor ever cease to be haunted by those eyes so full of the " vision of sudden death."

This letter is written in the intervals between the short periods of vocal exercise Signor O—— prescribes for me. The voice must take time to rest, but the interim it needs for that would be too brief for going out, so my letters are nearly all done between the sessions at the piano. For all merely technical work I stand by the instrument and touch occasional chords or notes, sitting only for the study of *solfeggi* and songs. The voice grows noticeably stronger, but the " veiled " notes in the middle get no clearer, nor do I get the brighter *timbre* in the upper region which I feel sure should characterize it. In the meantime it is useless to ask the maestro for any opinion about the future, for he certainly could not truthfully give a good one. If my strength increases (and there is sore need of it), it will soon be easy to tell if any solid benefit is gained from his teaching.

Two acquaintances of mine made their first appearance here recently in " La Sonnambula." The soprano, an American lady who had sung the opera many times before, has a light, but brilliant and flexible, voice. In spite of a totally inefficient company she made a fair success—not only by reason of her very evident ability, but also because she had the sympathy of the audience. The tenor, who has a really beautiful light voice, and is gifted with the handsome face and graceful figure which exactly fit him for such parts as Elvino, was ill and ought not to have been persuaded to sing. His upper voice was, by illness and the chill of the theatre, entirely lacking its usual brilliancy of *timbre*, but the audience knew nothing of his condition, so he merely got through the evening somehow, in the last act scarcely even trying to sing. It is, dramatically, a most insipid, uninspiring rôle, but its lyrical demands upon the artist are great, as it requires a high, facile voice so well-posed as to be capable of doing securely the most delicate work imaginable.

One generally hears the sugary music of Elvino wailed forth in a wiry falsetto, sounding very much like the voice of a cat that is not at all well! But this tenor sang in thoroughly manly fashion what phrases he was able to sing at all, and is, though luckless upon this occasion, an excellent artist and also a bright, interesting man. You know how we laughed over somebody's famous saying, that " the human race consists of three divisions—men, women, *and tenors !*" Now comes caustic Dr. Hans von Bulow, who is credited with the terrible statement :—"A tenor is not a man ; he is an illness ! " Does it not seem as if the Creator, in bestowing the rare and beautiful gift of a fine tenor voice, would not often vouchsafe to have much of anything else done up in the same human parcel with it ? But when a tenor does possess brains and the determination to be an artist, what greatness is possible to him !

I do not fill my pages with descriptions of the natural beauties and art-creations of Florence, because you can read such in many books better done than would be possible for me, and I fervently hope you will read them. Without giving the first and

freshest of my time and strength to museums, picture-galleries, churches, palaces,
gardens, and other things here to be seen,
enjoyed, and loved, I do try to gain something from them all.   I wish it were possible to tell every student of singing who is
coming here, to prepare himself by reading
histories of Florence and the lives of her
great men, so as to be ready truly to live in
the mediæval as well as in the modern city—
to rest in the tranquil life of its present, and
to draw constant inspiration from its mighty
past.

Surely the time has gone by when the
singer may content himself with merely
knowing how to do the mechanical work of
singing.   That leaves him an artisan—not
an artist.   No one, more than the singer,
needs to draw upon all Art and all Nature for
aliment for his soul and brain.   They feed
his imagination and give him power of conception.   I had access to few of the right
books before coming here, but for what
those few were to me I am forever grateful
to their writers, and to a dear friend in
whose library I found most of them.   They
have helped me so much to see with eyes

not quite material, and have made me feel the almost actual presence here, in their works, of the great ones of other centuries.

And not only is one made to know the presence of genius, but is forced to wonder at the spirit of art that filled the nation. Which is, after all, the greater marvel—that when the giants of those far days in the story of this Lily-Garden, those born in the perfume of its art-adoration, panoplied with its superb, self-forgetting, impersonal love of all art, stepped forth from the ranks to do great deeds, to shape from the Carrara blocks forms so noble and spiritual that millions have thrilled before their mute glory, or to shed holy light upon coming ages through enduring tints on the friezes and ceilings of her churches and palaces, and on bits of canvas and small tabernacles of wood, or to pour the molten metal into shapes of immutable power and beauty, or to lay stone upon stone, uprearing imperishable walls for the indwelling of the Holy Spirit or the fair body of man,—which, I say, is the greater marvel—that popes and princes reverenced their sublimity and bowed to their greater kingship, or that peasants and artisans lent loving hands to their mighty schemes, each seeking to learn well his own small task, and each doing it with the sweet fervour of one consecrated to a great use?

It is the one common end to which Florence worked—the devotion with which she, full-handed, poured out all things for the fulfilment of the rich commissions she gave to her Titans—that fills my soul with worship for her great days and great deeds. You will come here some time, so do begin at once to get the help which only books and study can give you in advance. Only by such preparation can one think deeply, reach down to hitherto hidden springs of feeling, and learn lessons no *maestro di canto* can teach.

We have often read and heard of the carnival revels in Italy—the last riotous festivities before Lent begins — but Florence is not prone to any great display or to any such mad merriment as is said to characterise the *festa* in some other cities, especially in Rome and Naples. For one thing, the weather at this season is too apt to be like that of New York, where I once witnessed a very ambitious attempt at a carnival procession. Ugh ! I shiver still with the memory of that dreary sky and bitter, piercing wind ! Ah, no ! It is something that must be wholly spontaneous—a wild fling of extravagant gayety which goes only with warmth, sunshine, and the first sweet breath of spring-time. Here, as in New York, there is much doubt as to whether rain, or even snow, may not fall and quench any effort to have a public and general display on Shrove Tuesday, so yesterday's was half-hearted and ill-organized, although it certainly afforded some diverting sights.

The streets were thronged with masqueraders. As the day chanced to be fine, hundreds of people seemed to have improvised costumes, and all others were in holiday attire, for at least there was no work done and few shops open. Carriages filled with people in ridiculous attire were greeted with shouts and laughs as they drove slowly up and down the Lung' Arno, where most of the crowd collected. One man was in a Mephistopheles dress with a salted codfish, tail downward, fastened to his back.

To-day all is quiet and Sunday-like. I bid fair to fast, whether I will or no, for it quite

escaped my memory to lay in supplies, and
even the thought of that salt fish is quite
tantalizing. You see I am in my new apartment in the Piazza Carraia, with T——— just
across the little corridor in a similar one.
Mine has a tiny kitchen, at the fittings of
which you would laugh. Then you would
find the great chimney-place and the rows
of brightly burnished copper utensils, and
all the glazed red-brown earthen pots, most
picturesque, and finally you would be puz-
zled and might well wonder how one would
go to work to cook anything.

Imagine standing almost under this immense chimney, and having before you a sort
of stone bench eight or ten feet long, and
about the height of your cooking-stove.
Near its top, two or three feet apart, are two
apertures cut into the front and extending
back perhaps a foot into the bench—just as
if made to slide drawers into. Over each of
these holes, at its farther end, is sunk into
the top a small square grate. Into that grate
you put a trifle of light wood, or a pine-
cone, with lumps of charcoal over it, and
then kindle your fire from underneath with
a bit of paper lighted and pushed into the

aperture until it is directly under the grate. So then you get a quick, hot fire which you easily rouse to greater activity by plying a straw fan at the mouth of the opening. The little smoke emitted by the charcoal goes up the yawning chimney above, and around or upon the grates full of burning coals you huddle your cooking-pots and pans. All the stone about each grate becomes heated, so your different dishes can be kept boiling or frying at high pressure, or may gently simmer at one side and keep warm for use.

I wonder we do not have such things in America to use in "summer-kitchens," especially where gas is expensive or unattainable. Any mason could construct one of brick or cement, with a smooth stone at the top—all at a small cost, and it is economical for fuel and easily kept clean. The only difficulty would be the chimney, and those here are often a sort of inverted half-cone of sheet-iron placed against the wall so that the smaller part at the top will just cover an opening into the chimney which is built into the wall. The great bench-like structure affords ample space for all the preparations for a meal which we usually spread out over a kitchen table. Of course I have not the time nor the experience regularly to keep house and cook all my meals, but upon moving into these rooms I was hungry for some real home-dishes, so for these ten days not a single meal have I taken at a restaurant.

You must know, however, that within a stone's throw of here, in some of the small, narrow streets like the Via del Moro, one can buy almost any food already cooked, so do not imagine I am perishing by a sort of slow suicidal process—poisoning myself with my own amateur cooking! No, but I can and do have oatmeal by paying a franc and a half for a small packet of it at a chemist's shop; and Indian corn (maize) is one of the cheap staples of food in Italy, so there is excellent "corn-meal" and the best results of my efforts therewith are some of the simple, easily made dishes we Americans miss so much in all foreign cookery.

The two other rooms which make up this little suite are very tiny, except in their upward extent. If they could be laid down upon their sides they would make rather large apartments. The cozy little sitting-room opens upon the Piazza Carraia, and gives me sunshine in the afternoon, and I can see the stream of people crossing the Arno upon the bridge—the Ponte alla Carraia, and hear the musical cries of the vendors of all sorts of things — papers, fruit, matches, wood, etc. One strapping fellow goes up and down the street, selling something the name of which I cannot make out, and uttering a strange cadence that finishes every time upon a high *A* of the loveliest *timbre* you can imagine. The only one of all the cries which has yet taken to my ear the form of words, I have got most comically wrong. It always sounds to me like " *Vado in cielo !* " and it does not seem likely that a peddlar of matches would be screaming out "I'm going to Heaven ! " Brimstone suggests quite a different destination !

These calls, though generally musical, are often so stentorian in the narrow streets that they need the mellowing effect of a little distance. To walk along by the side of a peripatetic vendor of matches, oranges, or cat's meat is sometimes to be stunned by the terrific force and volume poured forth by Signor Leatherlungs ! Just as I was turning into my door this morning and congratulating myself I was in time to escape the next outburst from a little, wiry, dark fellow with a rose in his mouth and a basket of lemons on his head, he took out the floral stopper and let loose. I thought the houses would fall even as the walls of Jericho fell by an assault of sound. To be so close to the fellow as he shouted, in a place that resounded like the inside of an empty cask, was something of a trial to the tympana of one's ears.

LETTER IV

LETTER IV

Villa Rinaldi, Val a' Ema,
Palm Sunday, March, 188–.

THE temperate joy of this Lenten festival suits well the mood of one who has been ill and is just far enough on the road to recovery to feel like creeping out to shake hands with the spring, and to promise himself that its increasing warmth and brightness will help him rapidly onward to renewed strength. To no one as to an invalid convalescing, can the smell of brown earth freshly turned by plough or spade, the perfume of growing things, the exquisite green of young leaves, and the discovery of the earliest primroses, crocuses, and daffodils, bring such revivifying pleasure.

63

The rooms in the Piazza alla Carraia proved to be unsafe, but the mischief was done before it could be helped. There is an old well under the house, and from a little door in one of the walls, I let down a bucket to draw up water, but must have also pulled up microbes, for after some days of unaccountable languor and heaviness, I developed a severe attack of some miasmatic character, so was brought out here, to his house, by my good friend, Baron von O———. With the kindest care and attention all is well now, and in a few days more I shall be able to go to the seaside to complete my cure. Pray do not get the impression that Florence is generally unsafe. It is quite out of any malarial district and the municipal water-supply is abundant and of the purest quality, but here and there is an old house, like the one I was in, where there is an ancient *pozzo* still in use, and of course that might be the case in any city of Italy.

The Villa Rinaldi is a house across the valley from the famous monastery called La Certosa. From Florence one leaves the Porta Romana and passes southward through the little village of Galluzzo, crosses the

brawling, rattling little Ema—the streamlet
which gives its name to the valley,—and
then, instead of ascending the bold height
upon which stands the picturesque Certosa,
one turns abruptly to the left from the
bridge, up through a field which slopes to
the Ema. The house is built upon a terrace
and is of ordinary size. There is a court
behind it containing a small, sheltered garden, with lemon-trees in huge earthen pots
and a high wall overrun with vines, and into
the wall is built a fountain fed from some
spring in the higher ground beyond. From
the front of the villa the view across the valley is lovely, with the curves of the brook
shown by the rank verdure and the yellow-
green willows, as well as by glimpses here
and there of its rapid current now swollen
by recent rains. The village of Galluzzo
with its long main street and large, open
piazza, nestles in sunny coziness between
the swells of the hills, and all about are the
white and cream-tinted villas, with high-
walled gardens, olive-groves, and trellised
vineyards.

There is an old grand piano in the *sa-
lotto*, but by weakness my voice is reduced

to a mere thread. It is hard to endure with patience this break in the routine of study, but perhaps the enforced rest will prove to be the very best thing for my singing. The lessons were going on pretty well, but I never seemed to acquire any increased power of endurance. I could not sing long at a time, and now that all is in retrospect I am sure it is only because the voice was not getting placed so as to stand hard work. I practised the scales and *solfeggi* given me in the earlier lessons, but often in the later ones Signor O—— did not call for them, and heard me only in songs and arias instead. I aimed to prepare with voice and fingers for each lesson so as to sing *da memoria* all the work given me to do. Aside from the benefit of exercising one's memory, it is a good thing to be freed from the necessity of looking at notes and words —by doing which one loses the helpful hints and signals a good teacher can always give, even while the pupil is actually singing.

Owing to the difficulty of learning by heart the Italian words I felt somewhat overweighted in the last lessons because of the number of songs given me to study. Perhaps the most attractive of them was a setting by Campana of one of the Dante sonnets in which the poets set forth the divine charms of his Beatrice—the sonnet beginning:

" *Tanto gentile, e tant' onesta pare la donna mia.*"

The words alone are exquisitely musical, but they need something more than the simple form of rhythmic reciting to the charming accompaniment the composer has supplied. It is one of those poems replete with double meanings, and neither an ornate melody nor lavish harmonies would suit it; simplicity of treatment is needful, but there should be inspiration as well.

Did you ever note how rare it is to find well-balanced worth in both text and music of songs? Now and then we find a superb poem wedded to great music, as in the case of Schubert's " *Erl King,*" while Handel gives us an entire and magnificent aria to the unimportant four lines:

" *Si, tra i ceppi e le ritorte,*
La mia fè risplenderà.

No, ne pur l'istessa morte
Il mio fuoco estinguerà." *

You ask how I am getting along with the language. It is such slow work for me because I seem not to possess the knack of picking it up by ear. One of the other students here and myself are having lessons together from a well-known teacher, and of us two I am perhaps a trifle the more advanced. We shall probably separate soon, because I really can make rapid work with the grammar and am assured that my pronunciation is good. Believing that in the matter of a pure accent much depends upon the beginnings, I have only lately begun to do much talking. There are plenty of people who say to students : " Now you must begin to speak at once wherever you are—with servants, shop-keepers, everybody." Excuse me ! I did not care to learn servants' and shop-keepers' Italian, and would do little in the way of conversing until I could tell pure Tuscan from the Florentine dialect, with its

* " Yes, amid the chains and tortures
  Shall my faith resplendent shine ;
  No, not even death's dark shadow
  Shall obscure that flame divine."

curious throaty scrape in place of the *k*
sound. The Italians are most helpful to a
beginner, giving him the aid of a word or a
gesture when he is at a loss to understand or
to speak, and if they ever laugh at the lin-
gual blunders of a *forestiere* they must do it
when he is quite out of hearing, for their
kindness and forbearance are remarkable,
and they must often be tempted to indulge
in something heartier than a smile.

I am obliged to study hard, not because
it is difficult to acquire a vocabulary and a
clear knowledge of the grammatical construction, but for a reason which is considered very unusual. It is that I have great
trouble in understanding the language when
hearing it spoken. It always sounds confused to me. People generally understand
a foreign tongue long before they can speak
it, do they not? With me it is quite the
other way about, and I make laughable mistakes through not comprehending what is
said to me. The chief difficulty encountered
by many of the students here is due to the
lack of a clear knowledge of their own language which would enable them to make comparisons between it and the Italian, and they

depend too much upon "picking up" the latter. If there is anything of special value in the "Italian method" of singing, it probably has much to do with the language, so one cannot afford delay in acquiring the free use of it.

I have had excellent lessons until coming out here, and besides keeping up the writing of exercises and the practice of reading aloud, I am finding some good opportunities for conversation. But it is a most elusive thing to me—*la lingua Italiana*. Some days it seems as though I were really getting a firm grip on it, and then suddenly something is said that leaves me stranded—without a word at command for answer. One digs away at the grammar, scribbles folios of exercises, and gets the dictionary all dog's-eared —only to find that half an hour's talk with a well-educated Italian is of more practical value than all. Yet, of course the study prepares the way for the greatest benefit from conversation. Most Florentines—I mean the common people—speak in dialect, but they construct well ; grammatical blunders are rare. How they can manage all their pronouns is to me a constant mystery, yet they do—even the least educated people.

The value of the Italian language to the student of singing can scarcely be overestimated. You will hear many say it is because of the frequency of the vowel sounds, but that is not so much the essential as is the simplicity of the vowels. That is what makes Italian a downright need to the student. It stands as a stepping-stone between the strictly technical work and the use of the more complicated and vigorous tongues, like English and German. I cannot see how it is possible for anyone to learn to sing well and to make the utmost of his voice without using this language as at least a phase of study. And, as has just been hinted, it is not so much the fact that it contains practically but the five vowel sounds represented by the a, e, i, o, and u, but that there are no " compound vowels " to mislead the student and constantly disturb the throat.

I say " practically," because the slight modifications in the e and o sounds are easily learned when the language becomes familiar. The main thing is that all the vowel sounds are simple in construction and do not include the "vanish" which is required to give a clear ending to so many of the English vowels, and which gives the throat an upsetting kind of twist just when it should be most completely in repose. For instance, our "long" sound of a is represented in Italian by e, and sounds simply like "eh," while in English it is expressed by "eh-ee." Unless one prepares for it by learning first to sing in Italian, there must be for the student a constant and confusing mental analysis going on in English singing, in order to extricate and use the pure, singable portions of the vowels. In German the diphthongs and modified vowels make similar trouble, if they are attempted before the voice is well settled in the use of simpler sounds. That done, German is wonderfully pungent and forceful to sing.

LETTER V

LETTER V

Viareggio, May 7, 188-.

I CAME down here on the first day of
the month. An entire change of air
seemed to be necessary in order to get
my strength back again. The journey was
a pleasant one in the bright spring weather.
At Pisa I stopped for three or four hours to
see the famous cathedral group—only time
enough to run about a little. I ascended the
Leaning Tower, went over the great church,
and then passed on to the Baptistery to see
the beautiful pulpit carved by Niccolò Pisano
and to hear the echo which is given from the
cone-shaped dome. The old *custode*, following his usual routine in showing visitors

about, snarled out a horribly nasal sound
which was sustained and repeated for a long
time, and was going to repeat the performance when I motioned him to wait. Taking a deep breath, I sang the tones of a common chord upward and downward, ending
upon the first of the octave, perhaps thus:

The effect was astonishing. Like a powerful organ diapason the chord sounded on
and on, scarcely seeming to diminish for several seconds, and being audible for a minute
or more. How wonderful to think that those
vibrations are still going on somewhere!

This is not the best season—in fact it is
about the worst—for seeing Viareggio. The
weather has been almost incessantly rainy,
but I have enjoyed the dripping, fragrant
pine - woods, and am most comfortably
housed in a small hotel which was once the
residence of Pacini, the composer. His
best-known opera, "Saffo," I have heard
but once, and shall not repine if henceforth
it is my fate to hear others instead.

I have not tried my voice for ten days,

but it will probably bear steady work now, and I am anxious to get back and make a trial with some other teacher than Signor O——. It is long since I have told you anything in careful detail about my lessons with him, but you know that in spite of my determination to have all possible faith in him and to afford him every chance to help me, I could not feel satisfied with his manner of teaching me. Of course my lessons were interrupted by my illness in March, but last month I stayed in town the greater part of the time, at the Pension C——, and had them as regularly as the maestro would give them to me. He certainly has great ability, but perhaps because of my fluctuating strength and the consequent unreliability of my voice, I have not been able to interest him sufficiently to secure his best efforts. My lessons grew shorter and shorter, and there was constantly decreasing endeavor upon his part to put the voice into better pose. Once all I did was to read two new songs—mere trifles—and then at the next lesson two more, without even a hearing of the first two. It is evident that I must find another teacher if anything is to be accomplished. Of that you shall hear when the change is actually made. I return to Florence to-morrow.

Villa Rinaldi, May 9th.

Upon my return, late yesterday afternoon, I found that Baron von O—— had asked several of the artists out here to dinner—was, in fact, like Hans Breitman, going to have a " barty.'' The whole villa was fragrant with lilies and early roses and had a festal appearance. And while the gastronomic arrangements had received his careful attention, they were far from representing all of the host's thoughtful hospitality. In my room, which opens from the dining-room, he placed young Signor S——, a blind pianist whose genius is well known here, having engaged him to play to us during dinner. Ordinarily I detest having music as an accompaniment to a banquet. If it is good it is too good to use merely as a stop-gap for lagging conversation, or to add to the sensuous luxury of a feast.

But, in this case, it was simply the crowning joy of a delightful evening. It was so good that it put all grosser pleasure well into the background, and helped to bring out the very best imaginings and expressions from the company of artists grouped about the table. It made the talk wholly profitable—all of it now and then ceasing in a happy silence when the splendid Bösendorfer grand gave forth something of especial beauty from under the facile fingers of the sightless player. I am sure we did not allow him to feel that the treasures of his art were wasted upon gourmands. We did not ask him for the greatest of music, which would have required from us the closest attention. Romantic and emotional things were more fitting, and those we had in profusion and perfection. Never have I heard played with such tenderness and beauty of expression the Chopin Nocturne, No. 2, of Opus 9, the exquisite melody beginning:

We had besides that a Chopin waltz given in just the right degree *capricciosamente,* and

four of Liszt's pieces, the two famous fantasias on " Rigoletto " and " Faust," a taran-
tella, and, finally, the deliciously exciting
"Regatta di Venezia." You see there demon-
strated the Italian fondness for Liszt. He is
the demi-god of the piano in all Italy, and
our astonishing blind boy played these things
with the most concentrated romantic passion.

It is probable that generations must pass
before Liszt will have his due recognition
as a writer for the piano. It is not that he
is difficult to comprehend. On the contrary,
no modern writer is less obscure. The difficulty lies rather in the confusing diversity of
his brilliant gifts. First he dazzled the musical world by the meteoric splendor of his
playing, and naturally enough that world expected to find in him no further and greater
creative quality. Then when his operatic
fantasias became known, like the two in
the programme above, with their alternately
delicate and titanic treatment of well-worn
themes—and also the Hungarian Rhapso-
dies—it became the fashion to believe him
incapable of more original and profound
composition. Yet there is a great library of

his works, large and small, which are still comparatively unknown—among them at least one picturesque and powerful sonata. No, the full measure of his many-sided genius may have to be learned after the witchery and passion of his playing shall have become only a tradition.

After we had risen from the table, and while the room was fast filling with tobacco fumes, we suddenly heard from the little walled garden the delicious thrum of strings. Almost at once we, who were dwellers in the Val d'Ema, knew what it meant. The village, like most Italian hamlets, has its small band of guitar and mandoline players, and knowing that we were having a *festa*, they came up the hillside to surprise us thus pleasantly. To hear such music sound out so unexpectedly upon the May night from all those throbbing strings was like an ecstasy, and the friendly young Italians could not have devised a better treat for us. After some concerted piece in which the mandolines twittered and sang over the rich chords from the guitars, there was a moment's silence followed by our applause. Then came a brief symphony and a light lyric tenor of beautiful *timbre* sang one of the most romantic of the Tuscan *canti popolari* :

> " *Dal dolce sonno svegliati,*
> *Donna del mio pensiero ;*
> *In sogno lusinghiero*
> *Cara, ti strinsi al sen.*
> *L'ore notturne passano,*
> *Passano i mesi, gl' anni,*
> *Restano sol gli affanni*
> *A lacerarmi il cor.*

> " *Se di tua voce flebile*
> *Non posso udire il suono,*
> *Ingrata !   Io t' abbandono !*
> *Più non m'udrai languir.*
> *E se un rivale in giubbilo*
> *Ora ti trovi al lato,*
> *Pensa allo sventurato*
> *Che morirà per te.*"

I cannot tell you what an entrancing effect this little serenade had upon us who listened. It was added like a caress to the beauty of the night. The last of it we heard as the young men passed down through the *podere* on their way back to the village. It sounded faintly back and kept us all fascinated until the night - breeze brought us the final soft repetition—

> " *Che morirà per te.*"

To-day I am considering about lessons,
but do not think it will be best to begin
with anybody until I shall have had a little
time in which to work my voice and get it
strengthened by daily practice after all this
period of inaction. My illness has left me
so weak in the muscles which control the
breath that I have no sustaining power ; the
apparatus collapses with the first effort.
Walks will soon strengthen me, and this
morning the first of them was taken up the
hill behind the house — such a lovely,
wild way, half path, and half cart-track.
Upon the small plateau past the crest of the
hill is a great villa with the arms of some
noble family emblazoned over the door, and
in front of it one of the prettiest sights I
have yet seen in Italy—a field of *trifoglio*
in bloom. You know what it is to see the
wind stirring into billows of soft, dull pink
our meadows of clover ? Well, imagine a
larger blossom of dusky, terra - cotta red,
growing rather taller and moving more flex-
ibly to the pressure of the breeze, and glow-
ing more and more intensely while you look,
as the wave passes over the field and comes
nearer. I am learning to love the olive-

trees, though their gray makes a sad note amid the fresh greens of spring. All winter the bare trees have looked to me stunted, dreary, monotonous, but now, clad in its shimmering mantle of foliage, the olive becomes a tree full of unique and fascinating character and a tenderly dominant tone in the landscape. Its lace-like shadow, whether cast by sun or moon, has a witchery and grace all its own.

Oh! speaking of beauty allied to sadness, I have been forgetting to tell you of a scene I witnessed here in April. It was when the sweet, humid, odorous night was over the hushed valley, and the soft gleams of the stars pierced the darkness only to make it mystic with faint thrills of light. Overwrought with exciting study, restless with surges of longing for intangible things, aching to be taken from my own self and self's vague miseries, I stepped out from the little *cortile* of the villa, and almost without cognizance of my dreaming senses, my feet took their way down the slope, through the field of whispering, half-grown grain, to the village. Beyond the bridge, the white walls of the little *trattoria* on the high bank above the chattering stream were luminous in the strange half-light, and the somewhat squalid village had a soft beauty and grace which my eyes had never been able to see in it by the less sympathetic light of day. Far up the one long street, on the broad piazza which bears—I forget now what resounding title—I could faintly discern a crowd of people moving turbulently to and fro, as if with some suppressed excitement and in the expectation of an unusual occurrence. There were no cries, and even the talk seemed hushed to a tremulous murmur, too confused for me to make out anything intelligible as I approached the throng and mingled with it.

As it was not in consonance with my mood to ask questions, I waited in silence, strolling through the wide square and noting here and there in the crowd odd charms of face, costume, and manner. The mystery was soon cleared by evidence that we were in the presence of the profoundest mystery of the world. The throng had gradually compressed itself into a solid, dark mass, but, as if pushed gently from the farther side, it parted silently, and the long-robed figures of the Misericordia came on, accompanied by eerie, fantastic shadows cast by the torches borne on either side of the little band. Voiceless and faceless (for they were, as usual, masked by their curious robe), they came abreast of where I was standing, and then I could see that they were followed by a double file of the village maidens, all in white garments. After them came, borne high upon the shoulders of young men, a coffin. O strange and sorrowful and beautiful sight ! It was another Elaine in her rose-hung boat —for I saw over the surrounding crowd which appeared to surge as billows do, and which seemed rocking it upon their unsteady level, the barque in which some mortal clay was floating by on its last, sad pilgrimage. As if to complete the illusion, festoons of flowers fell over its dark sides and seemed, to my fancy, to drip into the human stream.

Meeting one of the young musicians, the dark-eyed, slender Lello, who sang the haunting romanza last night, I soon learned that Elena—the loveliest of all the village girls, was being carried to her burial by night, in accordance with Italian custom. By some subtle side-current I had been drawn into

this river of humanity, and was seeing one
of the sweetest, saddest sights of a lifetime.
Sweet it was by reason of its delicate, suggestive picturesqueness, and for the tenderness exhibited by all that hushed, reverent
throng as the maiden's body was carried by
upon the shoulders of her sturdy playmates,
attended by her loving girl-friends, and es-
corted to the burial-ground by the faithful,
solemn devotees of charity in their white,
priest-like robes. In the silence one could
think out the mute story of human struggle
so soon ended, and in the darkness see a
vision of hands softly folded—of eyes closed
in peaceful, dreamless sleep. Perhaps never
again shall I see, in such mood to see and
to remember having seen, so perfect a picture in so perfect a setting as was made for
it by the soft mystery of that moonless night.
Nor need I see it again. The perfume of a
rose, the glint of a star, the rustle of a priest's
robe, the yellow flare of a torch, may bring
it back to my eyes any moment.

LETTER VI

LETTER VI

Florence, June 24, 188–

LAMENT not! Shoulder to shoulder and soul to soul with the composer, stands the interpreter. You think the latter's work is "ephemeral"—is done and then forgotten? Forgotten by whom? Ephemeral in what atmosphere? Ask the very remotest stars if even they may arrest the vibrations that start from us in a song. No— forever no! A song well made becomes only when worthily sung, a beautiful, imperishable reality. The other arts give us things embodied—"things which last," you say?

But does not the very fact that their beauty is bound up in material things make them less fine, far-reaching, true, and lasting than music? "The statue almost breathes—the portrait almost speaks—the painted clouds seem to move." So we speak to each other before great works, and what we mean is that the artist, in his material and impassable bounds, has been compelled to stop just short of where music begins. All that he could do was to reproduce what could be seen—copy what Nature had already given us lavishly. Motion and sound, which are one and the same thing, he could not portray with brush or chisel. These works of his are copies of dead things. Music deals with creation's imperishable soul. To the eye Nature has beautified herself with marvels that must decay, but audible Nature is a realm wherein only the laws are given to us, and they must be discovered and applied. We work directly upon the essence of creation—upon the cosmos itself.

Think far into this, and you will soon know how real song is. Speak to me of it out of your thinking, for there are so few of us who do help each other to these living

coals from the altar of eternal truth. If
singing is, as you say, "a breath," it is a
" breath of divinity and an instinct of the
beauty that is eternal in heaven." We gaze
into a printed book and we sing with voice
or fingers—and the machinery is set in motion to record somewhere both the sounds
we send forth and the intent we have in
sending them. Well it is for us that the
intention stands registered with the deed.
Truly, we should have a care what Thing we
cast into the Sea of Everlasting Sound, for,
be what it may, it shall displace the whole—
even to the last drops on the crest of the
wavelet in the farthest and loneliest cove.
And the ceaseless motion thence shall return
and track to its hiding-place the base and
worthless refuse or the shining jewel we threw
into those holy depths.

The figure is not a fanciful one. Music is
no humanly contrived affair. It is cosmic—
it is primal. I sorrow for the singer who
never feels that his voice goes straight to the
heart of all things visible and invisible, and
who cannot understand how distinctly creative is his art. No work in this world can
be made more worthy and more real. Em-

erson says : " The true artist has the planet for his pedestal." When the eye of man is freed from its grossness and limitations, to look into nature's mysteries and see what motion is to all substance and all sound, then shall the ear learn what a far, faint echo our best music is of that which is the essence of supernal motion.

But oh ! how difficult it is to keep the spirit looking to such heights and the hand upon the wheel of daily drudgery ! Here am I, talking to you from time to time out of the deeps of certain convictions, but almost powerless to exert them upon myself so as to compel my voice to do the things plainly needing to be done. Help me to greater patience and to the fuller understanding that the growth must be from without as well as from within. Speaking and working from the truths I consciously possessed, but could not fully exemplify, I have been able to help others to sing. But no one ever yet made himself a singer. There is a certain essential factor in the training which is represented by constant watchfulness, guidance, and criticism from without. Lacking that aid, I have never, up to this last month, learned even what *not* to do with my own voice.

After my letter, begun May 7th, life went on with me much the same as it had been doing all the spring. The enforced idleness caused by my illness was not wholly a bad thing, as it enabled me to reflect carefully upon, and to value properly, the work done since my arrival in Florence. My doubts as to whether it would be best to continue lessons much longer with Signor O—— were expressed to you from time to time, but when returning strength enabled me to resume work it seemed impossible, after all the hopes built upon him, to give him up without further trial. Therefore I resumed my lessons with him. I ought to add that there was also to influence me the feeling that the fault might not be his, but that by lack of physical power and consequently of good vocal condition, I had failed to interest him.

All things considered, the fresh start was taken. He pronounced my voice much improved by repose, and I am sure all would have gone well if he had but applied himself to the careful work of placing and delivering the voice. But the lessons were the same unsatisfactory affairs as before. It were folly to continue attempting to sing delicate *salon* pieces, with an occasional scena like the " *Vieni! la mia vendetta*," from "Lucrezia Borgia." I was strong enough really to work, even if I could not sing *a piena voce* for long at a time; and certainly, if my strength were sufficient for the study of songs and arias, it was ample for the far less trying business of " placing." No, it was useless to expect Signor O—— to help me lay the required foundation. Perhaps I ought to have asked him more definitely to do so, yet with the need so evident it is hardly likely that he would have heeded my request if he would not anticipate it.

But now for a month I have been studying with a really great *maestro di canto*, one whose greatness lies not alone in ability, research, and experience, but also in his earnestness and indomitable industry in his teaching. Just as I was feeling discouraged about finding the right master here, and was seriously considering whether it would not be better to remove to Milan, my best of friends here, Mr. T——, was making the acquaintance of several Italian pupils of Cavaliere Francesco Cortesi. Mr. T——— decided to go to him for lessons, but found it was one thing to make the decision and another to get the lessons. He had to make three visits with as many trials of his voice before Signor Cortesi would consent to take him—being vocally out of sorts and so perhaps seeming less desirable as a pupil than he really is.

It was not long before I also decided to try for lessons. My visit to the maestro was a refreshing experience. He made a most thorough trial of my voice in many ways, and with a great variety of exercises. I sang sustained tones, octave skips, *arpeggi*, scales in different forms, cadenzas, shakes, recitatives, and arias. He said little except to indicate each successive exercise, and seldom stopped me to make any corrections. It was clearly a trial to enable him to know what I had learned and what the voice was capable of doing. His manner was kind and considerate, even sympathetic. I was so conscious that his serious eyes revealed a process of earnest thought and such clear judgment, that it became to me both

easy and necessary to show him frankly all
my defects, whether natural or acquired.

I have since learned to know those eyes
and to be dominated by them, but this first
day they kept on for at least forty minutes of
inscrutability, storing up things to be spoken
when the ample trial should be over. He
then said : "Almost everything you do is
wrong, and it is impossible to predict now
what you will be able to accomplish, but I
have a curious feeling that there is something
worth working for in your voice, so if you
will begin with daily lessons for one month,
and will continue them for a second month in
case I think it necessary to do so, I will take
you."

His frankness, his complete disapproval of
my past work, and his stipulation for thoroughness, were refreshing.   He was very
busy, and the price he mentioned for the
daily lessons of one hour each proved to me
that the money consideration was little to
him.   If I was not in the Palace of Truth
(and it seemed rather like it to have the
moral shower-bath Signor Cortesi gave me !),
I was nevertheless in a grim, narrow, old
palazzo in the Via de' Ginori, not far from

San Lorenzo and the Medici Chapel—and am there now. But of that later.

An appointment was made and my lessons began on May 24th, just a month ago. I was still staying at the Villa Rinaldi, and all the country-side was so exquisitely love-ly with the beauty of the spring that it seemed impossible to leave the place. In the fields the scarlet fire of the poppies flashed forth when the breeze pressed down the level of the growing grain. Tumbles of honeysuckle were everywhere, and the grape vines in long festoons seemed to take hold of hands and dance down the hillsides. On the high walls the pumpkin vines clam-bered and put forth broad, fresh leaves, while the huge golden blossoms shone among the shell-tints of wild roses. Through all the soft April nights the nightingale in the ilex-tree near my window had often awakened me with the strange charm of its tender voice.

> " The singing of that happy nightingale
> .   .   .   .   .   did most truly
> Satiate the hungry dark with melody."

I liked living there in the quiet villa, in that most fertile and lovely valley of all the

Tuscan land. I liked my quaint room with its high canopied bed, the noble grand piano, and the writing-table always ready by the window over the garden. Baron von O—— was the kindest of hosts and an interesting companion. He taught me—words and music—some weird little Hungarian songs by playing them over on his violin and repeating the verses. I had, to share my walks, his big, beautiful Maremma dog, named for an old-time warrior of Hungary.

But the weather was growing hot, and while it was pleasant enough to go to and from the city by choosing one's hours for it, the perfunctory trips for lessons were beginning to tell upon me, and too often by the time I had traversed the dusty roads between the high walls that shut out the breeze and reflected to each other the rays of the mounting sun, I reached the studio fagged and out of voice. So the master advised me to come into town and stay.

I am sure he was right. While a singer can scarcely have too much exercise in open air, there should be no physical exertion just before singing. Only yesterday I left

the villa to come here and live in this old—
very old—house in the Via de' Ginori. Signor Cortesi's housekeeper, whom we who
frequent the studio all know as "Maddalena," and never think to ask her other
name, has charge of a floor two flights of
stairs below the one in which he lives, and
one flight up from the street. One of these
rooms I hired from her, and here behold
me established to live in veritable Italian
fashion. My room is the farthest one in
the rear part and has the whole width of the
house—which is not more than eighteen
feet. Going from it to the door which
opens on the stairway leading to the street,
is like taking a "constitutional," so long is
the narrow old house.

One window of this room gives on a small
court or air-shaft, down which Signor Cortesi calls to me whenever he wants me to
come up for a lesson or to hear some of his
pupils. The other window opens on a pretty little walled garden belonging to the next
house, and through it comes the fresh breeze
from the mountains past Fiesole. It is
pleasant to have an outlook upon this shady
bower with its glossy-leaved lemon-trees and

its tangle of jasmine and grape-vines. A big gray cat blinks solemnly at me from the wall, and seems almost a companion and contemporary to the weather-stained statue in the far corner. The birds twitter joyously about, and as I have seen no human being set foot in the fresh little nook it seems as if it were quite my own.

My room has a floor of well-laid red tiles, and contains, besides the comfortable bed, a large wardrobe, washing-stand, chest of drawers, chairs, table, sofa, and a small piano. I miss the splendid Viennese grand that was carried out to the villa for my use, but there is hardly room for it here. I make my own morning coffee in a French coffee-pot and have fresh rolls and excellent Milan butter, and with these take a little honey or fruit. A quarter of an hour later sees me at the piano for a half-hour of practice upon exercises. The daily lessons are proving my vocal salvation, and I have long since begged for a second month of them without waiting to know if the master considered it actually necessary.

LETTER VII

Technical Studies.—Uncertain Production.—A Desperate Remedy.—Paralyzing Effect of False Theories.—Benefit Derived from Daily Lessons.—Necessity of Gaining Flexibility of Voice. A Perfect *legato*.—Signor Donzelli and his Father, the Famous Tenor.—A Fine Tenor of To-day.—Breathing.—The *messa di voce*.—Cost of Living.—Foreigners' Prices and Italian Prices.—Cost of Lessons.

Florence, July, 188–.

NO description can do justice to the patience and painstaking care Signor Cortesi gives me in my daily lessons. Over and over the same ground we go in this, to me, delightful drudgery. His pleasure must be that of an enthusiastic teacher who loves best the satisfaction of seeing his pupils improve. My lesson - routine begins with the sustaining of single tones from upward chromatically through the octave. Then, beginning upon the same low *A*, comes the following exercise :  which is carried up to the *E* above the lines __Do__ __Fa__ __Do__ of the bass clef, and often to the *F* and *F-sharp*. The "f" of the syllable "fa" is firmly pronounced, the vowel sound seeming to spring into place after it. A light *portamento* from the upper tone back to the lower one prevents the nervous closing of the throat, which is apt to accompany the sustaining and leaving of higher tones. Then follow scales in different forms, but always beginning with one in which the downward run precedes the upward, as :

Ah   ah . . . .

The attack across the octave at the beginning of the exercise is to place the upper tone in exactly the right manner, so that the voice is able to return to it in the upward scale. My main difficulty in "placing" has been in getting a sufficiently bright tone—all my middle and upper voice being deficient in frankness. Doubtless you remember how I had been taught to sing "open" tones up to and thence upward to make "covered" ones. The quoted words are, perhaps, as good terms as any, but the trouble is that I had not learned how to *direct* my voice so as to keep any definite texture in it, and the result was that all the tones below the *C* were veiled, uncertain of intonation, and wholly lacking in character or *timbre*, while those above were forced into such pose as they had, and were quite incapable of modulation. In brief, there was almost nothing spontaneous and sure in my entire range.

At first, with habit and wrong ideas so strongly fixed, it was most difficult to get any tone freely and frankly delivered, but the maestro's patience conquered gradually. For several lessons that dreaded tone would come in the old way—dead in sound, devoid of all resonance. One Friday he said to me: "Now we can get no farther until that tone is given freely and clearly." That was enough for me to know. Taking a full breath I tore out the tone, doing something with it that convinced me that at least it was not impossible to get out of the old groove. The treatment was heroic, perhaps even perilous, but

it was radical and proved the maestro's point
—that the old ways could be broken and
changed. I did not sing again until the
following Monday, but was then able to go
on with less mental obstruction. No singer
can tell until he has been tried, the paralyzing power of false theories, and especially
those which are based upon what little we
can know of the muscular operations in the
singing throat.

The struggle with the middle *C* was not,
let me explain, for the sake of getting an
" open " tone thereon, but to wrench myself
away from old mannerisms of production—
things learned from so-called "scientific"
teachers. The particular trouble in this
matter was that I had been taught to press
the larynx down as far as possible. The result was the dull, veiled middle tones, and
no mental sense of directing the voice so as
to produce anything firmer and brighter.
Pressing the larynx down, forsooth! One
might as well attempt to cool this July
weather by pushing down the mercury in
the thermometer. Larynx, tongue, uvula—
all are perhaps in some measure indicators
of what is going on, but it is folly to work

directly with or upon them in order to place a voice. None of the teachers who muddle over anatomical matters in detail, and thereby create a distressing and hampering consciousness of muscular arrangement, ever turn out an artist—one who makes a really legitimate and successful career.

These daily lessons begin to show some good results. We have been working at Rossini music—not especially interesting in itself, but written to sing, and needing singing, too. Signor Cortesi maintains closely one of the beliefs of the old school—that many good things follow in the train of vocal flexibility. In spite of the either natural or acquired unevenness of my voice, he has made my scales fairly rapid and clear. They are sung very *legato*, with none of that bumping which a clever pupil of mine compared to " bricks tumbling out of a wheelbarrow ! " I note now that the trouble formerly experienced with the downward scale was largely due to not keeping the breath-pressure upon it. Apparently the pressure was needed only in the upward scale, and as soon as the descent began I let the muscles relax, and the consequence was

a blurred, uncertain scale. It used to vex
me much not to be able to sing with clear-
ness and security the downward *volata* in that
phrase Mephistopheles has in his first scene
in Gounod's " Faust "—the one which is
usually extended up to the *F*, thus:

Un bel cava - lie . . . . re.

Now such straightforward bits of *agilità*
are quite easy, and they need be, for some
of the cadenzas I have to study in the Rossini airs make the above seem child's play.

It is often difficult to understand the maestro, and I should doubtless have lost many
good points of his instruction had not T——
kindly come to my aid and sat patiently
through some of my earlier lessons to inter-
pret for me the directions and suggestions
I could not comprehend. Then the maestro
has staying with him for his long annual visit
an old friend from Bologna who speaks excellent English. He is no less a personage
than the son of Donzelli, the famous singer,
who with Mario and Rubini, made the trio

of the greatest tenors that ever flourished at one period. This Signor Donzelli, who is elderly, has been a fine singer—a baritone, but is a business man and has never made singing his profession. He has been, and is still, most kind about explaining to me, in his careful English, the things I might otherwise miss in my lessons.

Concerning his famous father, I must copy for you a few lines from Ellen C. Clayton's book, " Queens of Song." They occur in the very interesting chapter about Rosamundi Pisaroni, one of the greatest contraltos ever known : " The tenor was Donzelli, a Bolognese, at that time (1829) thirty years of age, and who had sung for some years in Italy. Mercadante had written for him his opera of ' Elisa e Claudio.' At Vienna, in 1822, he had produced a sensation which attracted the attention of the directors of the Théâtre Italien in Paris, who engaged him, and he had come from thence to London. His voice was a pure tenor of great compass, capable of much variety of inflection, and he possessed musical taste and discrimination. There was a fulness and richness in his tones, and an equality in his high and low notes which rendered his singing unsurpassed in smoothness and beauty."

There! Does it not picture to you a sweet, perfect cantabile, far different from the jerky, explosive singers of the modern stage? And the son of this great artist is now my elderly "guide, philosopher, and friend."

In the studio, a tiny room containing sofa, table, bookcases, and a small piano which is .always kept carefully in tune, I meet, now that the operatic season is over until autumn, artists well-known in all Italy, who come to Florence to resume study with their old master, or to "pass" new works with him. One of them is Sani, who has the next hour to mine. He is in person hardly the ideal tenor for Faust, Romeo, Manrico, Edgardo, etc., but the Italian public cares little for that. He sings—that is the main thing. *"Canta divinamente—come un angelo!"* That is the phrase the critics often employ concerning him, and it is truth. That strong, sweet tone seems to float with seraphic ease and freedom from his lips, swimming away upon his breath, so high, so pure, so true, and with the quality that warms the heart and fills the eyes. Sani is having a fine career in Italy and does not care to go far abroad.

Among the Italian students starting upon the stage is Silla Carobbi, a baritone. He is a short, stout man, with a fine head set almost neckless upon a broad, thick torso, and he possesses a voice which would be a *tenore robusto* if voices were to be classified merely by their range. It is really an exceptionally high baritone, somewhat hard and occasionally inclined to throaty quality, having little force in the lowest register, but pealing upward, trumpet-like, with splendid, ringing power. His singing is so full of passion, so replete with the *accenti caldi* which Italians love, that his career is sure to be a good one. I am apt to envy him and Sani their superabundant strength. While I now feel fairly elastic and buoyant, it is easy to see that the engine for this work —the breath-controlling muscles—is not with me as with them, all-sufficient for carrying the tone. One must be very strong to hold the voice to broad, sustained singing, and even stronger for delicate work—the *finesse* of vocal art.

In all art, whether that of the chisel, the brush, the voice, or in the playing of any musical instrument, do you not think the greatest finish and delicacy are born of the greatest strength ? It seems to me so. First comes the rude power, and then the ability to compress it and restrain it to the finer uses, gradually enslaving it to the will and making it respond to the subtler demands of the artist's dominating soul. Let a healthy person intending to study singing lie prone upon his back and have weights piled upon him. You know how much the naturally strong intercostal and abdominal muscles would sustain. But let him rise and attempt to sustain swelling tones, controlling the breath with those same muscles, and you will hear ragged, uneven sounds. The muscles that have all that crude power of resistance need special training to make them move with slow, steady precision and not waste the breath by spasmodic action. But the more power there is in reserve the more readily will the student acquire the finer control of it.

Mr. T—— is also having daily lessons. He needed them much, but his troubles differ from mine and are more easily dealt with. They are more mechanical—not so inextricably mental as mine. Then he has greater physical vigor, and almost at once he learns to sing a perfect swell, which is to me so difficult and so beautiful. He sends the tone out increasing roundly upon the breath and draws it back to a fine *piano*—an almost perfect *messa di voce*. I know that to accomplish this means to have the sensation of pressing the tone down, as if the breath were above it, pushing it downward, but the simple fact is that the process is beyond my present bodily strength. It will not always be, and it is not a bad thing to have the seal of confirmation set upon one's knowledge, even if the ability to use it practically is wanting.

Half truths grow into whole ones, and with them I get added powers of illustration, so that, as Signor Cortesi continually tells me, I shall be able to teach to others the things perhaps not fully attainable by . myself. It is surely one thing to sing well, even powerfully, and another to be able to endure the exacting work and the hardships of the life of an opera or concert singer. I shall learn to sing well, and if I must be content to know more than I can do, the teacher's field is always open to me, and it is a very attractive one.

You may care to know how I live now and what it costs. Perhaps no foreigner can hope to manage here quite as cheaply as an Italian can, but certainly the other American students spend twice the amount it costs me to live in comfort. Most of them pay from fifty to one hundred francs per month for rooms—foreigners' prices! I pay twenty francs. The good Maddalena takes care of my room and is glad to do me any extra service for a slight fee. My breakfasts, which must be simple and slight in order to utilize the morning hours for study, cost me about fifteen francs per month, and I have two good, plain meals per diem at an excellent restaurant. For those I pay by the week—fifteen francs, with a franc every week to the *cameriere* who serves me. For luncheon they give me soup or maccaroni, then meat with vegetables, and then a choice of cheese, pastry, pudding, or fruit—all with abundance of excellent bread and good red wine. Everything is well-cooked and neatly served, and within those stated limits there is always an appetising variety of dishes.

I speak of the wine as " good," and it is good—for wine! but it is ever a mystery to me how anything so acrid and crude to the taste can be manufactured from such delicious things as grapes. They must take a deal of trouble to eliminate everything pleasing to the palate. Still, everybody drinks it freely and there is almost no drunkenness, so I swallow my Chianti, Barbera, or Pomino, with a clear conscience if a wry face, and wonder whether our Prohibitionists might not better promote the production of cheap wines in America rather than make political crusades against bad whiskey.

Well, now you have the principal items of my living expenses. To Signor Cortesi I pay one hundred and fifty francs per month for my daily lessons of one hour each. That amount would afford me in New York five lessons of equal duration, so saying nothing of the difference in the cost of living, you see one reason why students should come here.

My maestro—great and constant as is his

interest in all his students—is certainly especially kind to me. Thrice in one day sometimes am I summoned upstairs to go carefully over my vocal exercises or to hear some lesson which he thinks may be of help to me, and often I am placed at the piano to accompany some pupil while he himself walks about, smoking, and giving an occasional direction. If he is called away for a few minutes, I, knowing his routine now, continue from one exercise to the next, repeating when needful, and practically giving the lesson—frequently to some famous artist. It is capital practice for me, and as such the maestro intends it.

And if it seems like slackness or shirking upon his part, let me say that lessons of one hour each are the custom here, partly because it takes an Italian teacher an hour to give a half-hour lesson. They have none of our terrible impetuosity in work—none of our high-pressure speed in any of their vocations. I have sung in the little studio upstairs almost incessantly for an hour and a half, and at other times we have taken it very easily, stopping several times in the course of an hour to rest or to talk. In the busier season doubtless I shall have only the time to which our arrangement entitles me, but just now it is free-and-easy, and I am the gainer by it. Whoever engages an hour of Signor Cortesi's time may be sure that his voice will in that time be worked as fully as is good for it.

Signor Cortesi is such a handsome man! He is perhaps fifty-four or fifty-five years old, is short and rather stoutly built, has a perfectly clear, rosy complexion, with fine, luminous eyes, and well-trimmed gray hair and beard. He is known as one of the best of Italian musical scholars, and a successful composer of operas of the lighter type. He graduated early in life from the finest school of music in the country—that of Bologna—and studied composition with Rossini, who made all his pupils study the voice closely so as to write for singers as well as for orchestras. In another letter there will be more to tell you of Signor Cortesi's most interesting life and personality. *Addio per ora.*

LETTER VIII

LETTER VIII

Foreign Students in Florence.—Milan.—Broad Musical Culture for Singers.—A Fine Example.—*Le beau sexe.*—The Students of Painting.—Our Mutual Friend.— Hard Study. — The *mezza voce.* — Duet from "Semiramide" with a Danish Soprano.—At the Theatre.—Signora Eleonora Duse.—New Fields of Study.—"Ernani."—A Cadenza.—*Basso cantante* rôles.

Florence, July, 188-.

YOU wish to know something about the other foreign students here. There are not many in all. Milan is the place where perhaps four-fifths of the operatic engagements for Italy are made, and of course a great many artists are there engaged for other countries also. Therefore, nearly all the foreign students either go at once to Milan and do all their study in that city, or gravitate thither in search of "*scritture*" when they approach readiness for a public appearance. Lamperti, now very old, still attracts many students, and his is a name to

conjure with. Sangiovanni has excellent
artists all over the world, although it is well
understood that his specialty is the imparting
of style and repertoire rather than the more
difficult work of voice-placing.

However that may be, Milan has drawn to
itself the greatest number of teachers and innumerable agencies, and, as a natural consequence, the students flock thither. The
operatic seasons there are better than in
other towns, but here there is at least the
advantage of a much better climate. Situ-
ated upon an open plain, Milan is swept by
fierce winds in winter, and in summer is
baked and arid. The comparatively few students who come to Florence are commonly
influenced by the question of climate, or else
come here, as I did, to reach some special
teacher. There are less than a dozen American men studying singing here this year and
fewer still from other countries.

Just now all excepting myself are out of
town at mountain or seaside resorts, so while
their backs are turned it is a good time to
gossip about them. Possibly my friend
T—— is in Florence, but I have not seen
him lately, so quietly do I live in the warm

weather—and you know all about him. He
and I are the only ones who do not now
study with Signor O——, and it is rather
absurd but true, that the fact makes a difference in the treatment we receive from *les
autres*. From that charge I must except one
of them, Mr. W——, the son of a distinguished American singer. He is always the
same cordial and reasonable gentleman, one
with whom it is a pleasure and advantage
to associate. Why should others be less
courteous? Was I not right in changing
teachers when my own needs demanded a
change? My lessons were not advancing
me; I was getting nothing of the radical
and thorough treatment my singing needed.
I have no unkind feeling toward my former
maestro, nor do I criticise him upon general
lines. Have I not all along testified to his
great ability? He is the last one to care
about my having left him, or to care if the
others do likewise, for he can fill up all the
hours he wishes to devote to teaching with
amateurs who gladly pay him double the
professional fees. It seems to me exces-
sively silly for his pupils to take up a line
of defence for him when he cannot possibly

care in the least about the whole petty business.

Of them one has a voice of singular beauty, a mellow, round tenor which ought to come out well when he learns that study does not mean singing operas *a piena voce* for hours at a stretch. He will never do much serious work ; comic opera has marked him for her own and should pay him handsomely. There is a basso with an excellent voice, but he will drift easily back to business life, perhaps singing usefully in a church choir. Then there is another tenor whose voice is at present quite unformed. A baritone whom I know is to arrive soon. He has a good voice but shows a trouble too common among the students—a lack of technical knowledge of the science of music. Too many such have not the habit of application to study which would carry them to broader and firmer ground, and without it they must surely discover that the special training will come to an early stop. The superstructure must be uncertain while the foundation is not deep and broad.

Of all here the most thoroughly prepared to become a singer is the Mr. W—— of whom

I have spoken. He is a deep student of harmony, having here in Florence the exceptional advantage of study with one of the ripest musical scholars of Great Britain, Dr. A. C. Mackenzie, and he has a real gift for composition which should be utilized. He is an excellent pianist, as I lately learned by hearing him play, with Mrs. C—— at her hospitable home, the " Préludes Symphoniques " of Liszt. His voice is a rich basso, with a compass that brings within its scope rôles like Marcel in " Les Huguenots " and Sarastro in " Il Flauto Magico." He has been here three years with Signor O—— and when his upper tones are placed he will sing splendidly.

The only English-speaking ladies of whom I can tell you are Miss C—— and Miss Mc-D—— and they are both non-professional students. The former has a lovely contralto voice and sings with the truest feeling when she is strong enough to sing at all—for her health is quite delicate.

Miss McD——'s artistic singing is one of the chief resources of entertainment in Florentine society. She is too serious in her study to waste voice and strength long by letting them go freely hand in hand with extreme amiability. With a round, full-toned mezzo-soprano voice of deliciously sympathetic quality, with much personal beauty and the rarer charm of a simple, earnest manner, she will soon find herself where the field will broaden and afford her ampler scope than drawing-room singing. It is a thing good in itself, but as a finality scarcely worthy of an artist. That Miss McD——— is rapidly becoming, and if she shall some time decide to sing professionally, many will rejoice to have the artist-guild enriched by the entrance into it of one who is by birth and education so thoroughly a lady.

The " painter-boys," as we commonly style them, are, taken collectively, much more interesting than are we of the sister-craft ; and as they have much influence upon the lives of the " singing-boys," and many common interests with them, it is not amiss to speak of them in this connection. So entirely the first and foremost, that except when one considers his jovial spirit of *bonne camaraderie*, he should not be included in the student category, is D———. He has a school outside the Porta Romana, and is the teacher of the "boys," as well as leader in all their frolics. It was his powerful, magnetic personality, which, rebelling against the cold, academic spirit of the Munich school, drew away from it, with his own secession, many of its students. They followed him to Venice, and later several of them came here with him, and it is quite the fashion to speak of them as "the D—— boys." So, although he is scarcely at the entrance of middle-life, it is not fair to class him with his pupils and followers. He has a grand head, with a grave German face, although I believe he is quite as much American as thousands of others, *i.e.*, by the "accident of birth." I know little of his painting, and would be an incompetent critic of it, but I have a feeling that he will be best known as an instructor, in which place he will show the qualities that will always inspire his students to work with ardor toward the highest aims. A man with a face like his—somewhat heavy in repose — but with eyes that can fairly blaze in response to any art-enthusiasm will not only go far himself, but will have the strength to carry others onward with him.

I shall never forget my first meeting with

him. Entering one early evening the little *trattoria* where many of us were accustomed to meet at dinner, I was all aglow with an entrancing effect of light I had just witnessed in the church of Santa Maria Novella, and without noting the presence of a stranger at one end of the table, I rushed into a description of the scene. As I ended some one introduced me to D——, who had just returned to Florence after a prolonged absence. What do you think he said? Nothing much, but the way he darts his glance and thumps out his words is like an electric shock. "You paint? No? Ought to!" It sounds too much like telling it to my own credit, but it is really only to show you how the man flames up when anything kindles the soul in him. It is not unlikely that his very presence, all unapprehended as it was by me, lent me a bit of unaccustomed fluency and eloquence.

Another personality, more steadily sunny, and perhaps the most popular of all, is that of R——, also a German-American. He is refreshingly original, and has blue eyes full of little dancing, rollicking devils! Yet his nature is so many-sided and so impressible that those same eyes are not ashamed to show themselves humid over the ineffable beauty of a sunset or of a tender strain of music. His influence over the singing-students is the most marked of any, and I am often furious with him for not exercising it more for their good than to give vent to his limitless enthusiasm and really do them mischief by unqualified praise. A touch of feeling in the turn of a phrase, and more often some merely sensuous beauty of tone, and R—— is prone to be unrestrained in his praise just when his powerful individuality combined with his high ability as a musical critic would enable him to say the "word in season" without stinting his approval of what is really good. As a painter he will perhaps be impatient of drudgery, and will not soon acquire the needful technique, being a determined "impressionist," but he is capable of the noblest things, and, as the French say, he will "arrive." No one among them all so interests and fascinates me as R—— not even excepting D—— himself.

Of the four or five others in the little studio school I do not now speak—partly because they are to me quite overshadowed by these two, and in part because I do not know them well.

Outside the professional circle, but very much inside the hearts of its members who know him well enough, is a clever young Scotchman who is in business here, and we often say that no artist or student of art could possibly have a more healthy, helpful, sympathetic friend than P——, "Sandy" we generally call him. Managing to offend no one by it, he chooses his friends carefully, but when once the choice is made it is to last, and no comrade can be truer or kinder than this same Sandy. I have had a chance to observe this, although my real acquaintance with him is recent. He and R —— came and breakfasted with me lately, and it is likely I shall have more to tell you of both later on.

My daily lessons go on steadily, and Signor Cortesi is as patient and unwearied as at the beginning. We are now finishing the second month, and if he consents I shall certainly go on with the same arrangement— daily lessons—for another month. The exercises are not varied much, and the voice has grown much freer and surer and more ringing. My one difficulty is the lack of bodily strength. Without that no one can sustain the work of singing an opera, nor can I, until I get much more power in the muscles that control the breath, hope to gain the use of a steady *mezza voce*. The simpler technical exercises take up most of each lesson, and the balance of the hour is spent entirely upon Rossini music. " Semiramide " was the first opera, and if you know Assur's *aria d'entrata* and that the maestro re-wrote the cadenza for me, doubling its length and difficulty, you will see what flexibility is needed for the part.

The duo with the Queen I had the advantage of studying with one of Signor Cortesi's pupils, a Danish soprano, Mademoiselle Rothe. Of her I have reserved special mention until now. She has a lovely voice, and he has certainly taught her to sing perfectly. The scale is faultless, every note round, pure, and easily uttered. With health she will make a good career, but at present she is far from strong.

Lately we have been at work upon the " Mosè " (" Moses in Egypt "), in which I study both parts—Mosè and Faraone. There is a difficult duet for tenor and baritone which it has been a great pleasure to study with T——. His voice, though light, is high and extremely flexible. The cadenzas are all made over and expanded for us, and some of the other florid passages made fearfully intricate. Well sung by two artists possessing voices of sufficient power and flexibility combined, the duet must have a most hair-raising effect. I was mistaken in saying we had used nothing but Rossini music—forgetting that I learned also the bass rôle in " I Puritani," though I cannot yet hold my voice in shape to do the light *legato* work of the song.

There has been an excellent company at one of the summer-theatres, the Arena Nazionale, and I went several times. The roof of the auditorium is raised from the walls so as to leave a ring of open space all around, which admits air and lets out smoke and the heat of the gas, so that the theatre is a popular hot-weather resort. The company is excellent throughout, and its members are evidently accustomed to playing together. The very best of the actresses is a rising celebrity in Italy, and rapidly becoming the formidable rival of Virginia Marini, who is often called the Bernhardt of Italy. This other one is Signora Duse, and I heartily wish you could see and hear her. She is a wonderful exhibition of what can be done by one to whom nature has denied great beauty of face or figure. Her voice is small, but managed with consummate art. It is not as bewitching as the Bernhardt's, which is also lacking in power, but, unlike the great French actress, Signora Duse always makes it last through the most exacting rôle.

Her versatility is only that of the whole company epitomized. They play a large repertoire and seem at home in everything. To see La Duse one night in the throes of such a part as Fedora or Odette, and the next fairly coruscating with gayety in Goldoni's comedy, " La Locandiera," is to see two marvellous women in one frail body. Her Italian is delicious music, so firmly and fully and so naturally does it sound forth— with the most fascinating *pizzicato* effect, or with smooth grandeur—as she wills and the part demands. You may care to know that a good seat in the Arena Nazionale costs me one franc thirty centimes, so considered only as lessons in the language the evenings are not expensive, particularly when there is to be heard such an exponent of *la lingua Toscana* as Signora Duse.

"Your voice is now large enough to sing music of greater breadth than Rossini's ; let us try something of Verdi's." That was what the maestro said to me directly after the technical exercises were over in to-day's lesson, and we began at once upon the "Ernani," in which of course I sing Silva, with its *cheval de bataille* for all the bassos —the "*Infelice.*" Upon first reading it of course I sang the florid cadenza written in the final phrase, although I knew that such are rarely used now. Some more dramatic peroration is generally substituted for those meaningless roulades, and for this cavatina Signor Cortesi wrote me the following, which seems to me an effective ending :

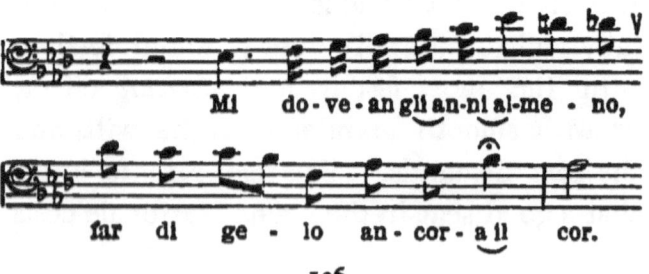

Mi do - ve - an gli an-ni al-me - no, far di ge - lo an - cor - a il cor.

You will have noted how often in the operas I study the parts for *basso-cantante* instead of those for baritone. The voice has mostly the texture and quality of a baritone, but not enough upper range—at least not so as to permit the free use of the tones above the middle *C.* The rôles for baritone are quite too high for me, although had I plenty of strength it might be possible to sing some of them. It must be remembered that when most of them were written and first sung the prevailing pitch was lower. It is a great pity that, through the efforts of makers of various instruments to make those wares as brilliant in tone as possible, such an extremely high pitch has been forced upon singers. It means for them great difficulties in true intonation and the management of tone-colouring, and an early decay of the vocal powers.

Thanks for the opera scores. When you come over to study, be sure you leave none behind. Many of the copyrights are owned here by publishers who hold them at almost prohibitive prices, so it is economy to bring over all the scores that can possibly be of use. I am so thoroughly enjoying these widened realms of study. The Rossini music was fascinating, and it was delightful to sing things written from the standpoint of sympathy with the vocalist, but the broader, more declamatory music gives me greater pleasure.

LETTER IX

LETTER IX

Repose from Study.—Viareggio again.— Effect of
Three Months of Daily Lessons.— Things Lacking.
—Good Health Needful.—Nava's "Solfeggi" and
two Ways of Reading them.—We have Resort to
Rossini again.—Signor Scheggi and his Method
of Teaching Acting.—In the *pineta.*—A Splendid
Military Band.—Unaccountable Lack of Good
Church Music in the Land of Palestrina.—Im-
posts.— *Povera Italia* !—The King and Queen.

Viareggio, August, 188–

IN the "Letters on Music," by Louis
Ehlert, this passage is to be found : —
"You would not believe how much it
renews a musician to hang up the keys of the
pianoforte and music-desk, and to hear no
other music for a time save that of the ocean
and the woods. The rustling of the woods
purifies one's inward atmosphere and nour-
ishes it with fresh oxygen ; the long-
breathed rhythm of the waves lulls the wearied
thoughts magnetically. Such a repose is a

sort of winter - sleep, and a return to life is the most cheerful of all awakenings.''

Viareggio seemed, as I read these lines, to call me with plash of wavelets upon its broad *spiaggia* and with soft sough of breeze in its lovely, dreamy *pineta*. *Eccomi !* I am lapped and lulled by soft airs and soothing sounds. The light wind swings away the plumy tops of the pine - trees, disclosing the deep azure of a perfect sky, and the swaying shadows are the rhythmic complement of golden sunshine. What joy to rest so perfectly after the past three months of close application to study. After a week of this I expect to return to Florence refreshed and vigorous for the work which it is to be hoped need have no interruption through the coming autumn and winter.

Signor Cortesi has been so good to me—labouring with the utmost patience and fidelity, giving me, at my earnest solicitation, daily lessons during the entire three months since the beginning of my studies with him.   As he has no need to do such hard labour, being rich for an Italian gentleman, and also as this daily going over the same ground must have been exceedingly dry work, I need be

most grateful to him. The result of our united efforts is shown in such access of breadth
to my voice that you would not recognize it.
Besides that, I have acquired much flexibility,
and withal, my singing is considerably more
free and open. The troubles which remain
are—and I hope he will yet set them right—
that I have small use of the *mezza voce*, and
that the upper tones never seem to come
with the ease and spontaneity which should
characterize them. He says those matters
will come along duly in the course of my
work, and with the increase of bodily vigour.
More and more clearly what I have been doing makes me realize that the perfect, ideal
voice is the outcome and the crown of a
healthy body—a beautiful efflorescence, so
to speak, and of course none but a healthy
plant can produce a perfect flower.

Oh ! have I ever told you what a comical
time the maestro had with me over the business of sight-reading? At the risk of repeating some part of a former letter, let me
tell you that one day, shortly after my lessons
began, he had me bring a copy of Nava's
"Solfeggi." Placing it upon the piano-desk,
he directed me to read the first study, " with

the syllables.'' You know if there is anything in music that I can do it is to read *a
prima vista,* so on we went to the end of the
first *solfeggio,* which was, if I remember, in
B-flat. Signor Cortesi looked a bit mysti-
fied but said nothing, and turned the leaves
over to a more difficult one in another key—
perhaps *E.* This one was read with fluency,
and then another in still a different key—
the good man's astonishment becoming mo-
mentarily more and more evident.

Finally he said he had never known any
one to read by that method—the ''mov-
able-Do'' system, — and had not supposed
it possible for anyone to become so facile in
it, even so as to recognize temporary transi-
tions into other keys than the one indicated
by the signature, and changing the syllables
to suit such modulations. He confessed
that he could not follow me in it, and you
know how impossible it would be for me to
read with the '' fixed-Do ''—that is, the Do
always upon *C*—because it would so completely upset all my habits based upon carefully acquired knowledge of intervals and the
association of certain syllables with those intervals. Therefore we were forced to give

up the *solfeggi*, but for weeks afterward it was his delight to make me read at sight for some pupil or visitor chancing to be in the house during my lesson. Instead of the Nava we had recourse to the brilliant, florid airs from some of Rossini's comic operettas, notably those in "L'Inganno Felice," and "La Pietra del Paragone." The scena in the former is one bristling with technical difficulties, ending as it does with a rattling polka movement at a fearful speed.

Signor Scheggi, the veteran *basso-buffo*, has given me a few lessons in acting. His teaching is a kind of parroting process for the pupil, but is lucid enough. We first took up the "Lucrezia Borgia," in which I knew pretty well the rôle of Il Duca. He taught me the successive scenes of the part, by the method I have mentioned—giving me each position on the stage, each pose, gesture, and inflection, and then requiring me to imitate him. There is exaggeration in everything he does, but if he can give me freedom in gesture and a certain breadth of style, perhaps it will help me in singing, and when the time comes I can modify what is exuberant.

Other parts followed in rapid succession—Rodolfo in "La Sonnambula," Silva in "Ernani," Plunkett in "Marta," etc.—all taught to me in precisely the same manner. I feel somewhat disappointed in not being taught any general and underlying principles which would help me more in the future and with all rôles; but this is Scheggi's way, and must be so accepted. He is a dear old man, and takes infinite pains with me. Although eighty years old, he still not only acts but sings! That is, he does the rattling, talky parts of the old comic operas. In the "Matrimonio Segreto," by Cimarosa, he is celebrated, and as he is engaged for a short season soon to come on in one of the smaller Florentine theatres, with that opera in the répertoire, I may see and hear him in one of his best parts.

I wonder how you would like Viareggio. Writing you from here last spring, there was little to describe because it was not "the season," and now it decidedly is. The place is Italy's Coney Island. It is far from fashionable, but the air is not only sweet and pure from the sea, but is rendered aromatic by the *pineta*, a broad belt of pine-woods stretching for miles up and down the coast, and at most points only a few hundred yards from the shore. To-day I sit with my "pad" of paper, from which I tear for you these scribbled leaves, in the *pineta* south of the village. It belongs to the Duchess of Madrid, whose villa is about two miles south of Viareggio, and if that noble lady, in addition to her kindness in keeping this pleasant woodland accessible to visitors, would only have some plain benches scattered about within its shady precincts, she would have a still greater meed of gratitude from me for one, because I do not like sitting upon the ground and wondering if one of those pretty green and yellow lizards will not presently dodge into my trousers leg! Were I staying long enough, a hammock would be the thing to have—to swing and dream in.

A splendid band plays every evening upon the beach where promenades all Viareggio. There must be quite sixty men—all in military dress—for the band belongs to one of the Italian regiments. They stand in a circle, facing their leader in the centre, and play magnificently for nearly two hours of the early evening. Their selections are mainly of lighter music, but include some of the best overtures. They certainly play the Strauss waltzes better than I ever heard them done, except by Theodore Thomas's orchestra. It was, from my first days in Florence, a surprise to find the Italian bands so complete in organization and so perfectly drilled. All their playing is apparently done *con amore*, and it is difficult to see how it could be improved. Sometimes, at military funerals in Florence, when it was impossible to get through the crowds so as to be impressed by any sight of the *cortège*, I have been thrilled to the heart by hearing the band-music—so it was not that I was first prepared to be affected by gazing upon the stately, solemn procession.

It often strikes me as curious that the Italians should be so fond of associating music with splendid civic pomp, and yet have so little in their churches. It seems as if their love of dramatic effect would incline them to use the ritual of the church as a vehicle for grand music, but as a fact, the church organs are often very poor and badly played, while there is rarely any good singing. How

curious such a state of things is in the land
of Palestrina, Pergolesi, and di Lasso.

In a recent conversation with a charming
old American lady who has lived here more
than forty years, I was particularly interested
in the comparisons her experience enabled
her to make with regard to her early times
in Florence and these present days.   She
said that the cost of living forty years ago
was less than half what it is now, and that
the difference was not entirely because the
prices then were so much lower than now,
but in part because the influx of careless
rich people—and especially Americans and
English—had made fictitious values for supplies.   There is some truth in the statement,
but it does not justly cover the ground and
show the reasons why living is now more
and more expensive.

Poor Italy !   She is so hardly placed in
Europe !   If her people learn to take at
times some small advantage of vulgar visitors who make all possible show of their
wealth, is it not the same in other lands,
and have not the travellers their own un-
wisdom or ignorance to thank for it ?   The
terrible drain upon the resources of this

country in order to keep up the army and navy, has not so greatly raised the cost of producing food, but when all foodstuffs are brought to market the reason why they must bring an increased price is made evident enough. One has only to stand for an hour by the Porta Romana, or any other city gate, and see the hard-working Tuscan peasants come there to be mulcted a few centimes on every bottle of wine, every dozen of eggs, and every handful of vegetables they bring into the city to sell. The soldiers stationed at the gate stop each little donkey-cart or wheelbarrow and, inspecting the contents, collect the impost. It seems like robbery—like "grinding the faces of the poor," yet perhaps the government must do such things to keep Italy afloat in the world's sea of finance. The taxes are frightful, but at any rate all the fault is not to be found in the Italian Government. If Europe were not possessed by a devil of unrest which compels her—for purposes of menace and possible protection—to keep in every separate nation armies and navies ready for war, this lovely land could soon be in happy and prosperous condition.

Alas ! things are bound to be worse before they will be better ; the end is not yet. The German states are unwieldy — France is at the mercy of demagogues—the Unspeakable Turk is on the verge of bankruptcy—Hungary burns for independence—Poland even yet dares to writhe under the heel of her tyrant—Russia, like a gigantic savage, awaits her time to strike—England is ready to defend a square inch of territory even while leaving a hero like Gordon to perish for want of prompt rescue — while Italy must perforce hold her place by taking the very heart's blood of her peasantry at every gate of every town. Her government doubtless make mistakes, for governors are human, but if each European nation had to-day upon its throne such monarchs as the great - hearted, generous - handed Umberto and Margarita, there would quickly be peace and prosperity everywhere.

These two are absolutely great because absolutely unselfish. They work themselves old and give themselves poor, and are a splendid reproach to most others. In all her troubles Italy never forgets to account herself fortunate in having this noble pair

as a pattern of pure life and lofty patriotism
for all her sons and daughters. The king,
at a whispered word, leaves his table to don
the strange robe of the Misericordia and
engage in some work of mercy among the
poorest. Is there a scene of calamity he can
reach? He is there with his money and his
example—his very hands to work with if
helping hands be scarce. Queen Margarita is, of all women, foremost in works of
organized charity. Her visits to hospitals
and schools and asylums are not casual and
ornamental. With her own hands and eyes
she examines the tasks and the products of
educational and industrial schools, and into
the kitchens of her hospitals she goes to see
that the poor and the sick have proper food
properly prepared. No show monarchs
these. They are workers for country and
humanity. Italy remade and in the rough
they took from mighty King Victor Eman-
uel, and theirs is the scarcely less heroic
task to hold up by lives of devotion to duty
the lamp of pure patriotism. Their example shames those who make politics a trade
—if such are capable of feeling shame. For
their people they live, and in the hearts of

that people their names and memory will be deathless.

Later I am going to tell you how much, in the face of fearful odds, this struggling Italy strives to do for musical art. She never forgets that she is the cradle-land of song, and the day will surely come when she will show herself a worthy keeper of the old high traditions.

LETTER X

LETTER X

Via Tornabuoni,
Florence, September, 188–.

UPON my return from Viareggio my
room in the Via de' Ginori was in
temporary use, so I was obliged to
put up elsewhere until good quarters suitable
for the winter could be found. For a few
weeks I occupied two rooms in an old house
near the Arno. During the hot weather of
the late summer and early autumn they were
admirable—a comfortable bedroom, and a
vast *salon* in which my voice resounded with

all the vigor of the entire male chorus in a German opera! They were on the third floor of a dim, still, old *palazzo*, and you know that means what we would call the fourth floor, because here the *pian terreno* (ground floor) is not numbered. There was an excellent piano, and an *accordatore* living in the house tuned it for me immediately, so that I could resume work as soon as I arrived. But do you not wish you could have your big Chickering tuned for sixty cents?

I was determined to have, for the coming winter, rooms with abundance of sunshine, and now feel well repaid for the delay before these were found. They are charmingly placed in an angle of a fine old house, so that my south and west windows open upon a little balcony and give me floods of brilliant light, and at present a little too much heat.

Of course almost the first thing to be done upon returning to Florence was to go to the little red-tiled studio in the Via de' Ginori. The maestro had not been out of town at all, and was looking as ruddy, fresh, and handsome as when I last saw him. He heard me sing, said the voice was better for rest, and on the following day we resumed lessons—daily ones again for a time, so as to be sure of going on in exactly the right groove. I already have ten rôles in which it would only be necessary to learn some of the concerted music in order to have them prepared for use ; yet it is doubtful if I could endure the strain of singing them constantly in a theatre. You see, I have not had thus far the kind of bodily strength which would enable me to save the voice in places where artistic effect and economy of power go hand in hand. It takes much greater strength to reserve the voice and hold it in than is required for putting it forth with fulness. This curious weakness must some time leave me and allow me to utilise what is being learned.

I have again engaged meals by the week in the excellent restaurant of which you were told in a former letter. The cooking is good, and so is the service excepting on each Friday. That is market-day, and the half-dozen rooms are then crowded by well-to-do country people who spend the day in town, selling their produce and buying supplies of various sorts. By going a little earlier to my lunch I get a comfortable seat and enjoy watching the throng gather. Those people know where to find good fare and sound wine, so their patronage speaks well for the *trattoria*. The water is known to be good everywhere in Florence, excepting what is drawn from old wells, and there is no need of using that, because the municipality furnishes a bountiful supply from the purest possible sources. It all comes from the streams several miles up in the hills, and is brought down through pipes to a tower near the Porta San Niccolò and thence is distributed over the city.

I must now leave this and do some study before going to my lesson. Would there were a chance of singing to you a splendid scena from Verdi's " Simone Boccanegra,'' which I have just been committing to memory: The recitative, "*A te l'estremo addio,*" with which it begins, is magnificent. The accompaniment is in Verdi's later style and is replete with richness and colour, needing an orchestra instead of the meagre resources of the piano. The brief romanza into which the recitative gradually goes becomes an impassioned *preghiera* with a very noble sweep to it and an especially grand phrase at the end. It is not written quite as I sing it, which is thus:

pre - ga, Ma - ri - a, per me,

The trouble is that the final *F* is, in my voice, too "woolly" — with not enough solid vibration in it. But you will remember that I never used to attempt anything so low as that, and also that when my throat was less free and open than usual, I could scarcely sing a steady *A*, the minor third above this note—so there is evidently some gain.

There is a matter of curious experience in study to relate. In the course of a recent lesson, my voice, while upon a sustained note, produced the *vibrato*. The maestro instantly remarked it, and said it could only come with the voice free from all obstruction in the throat, and warned me against yielding to the temptation to use it constantly. He must be right about its appertaining only to a free voice, for it seems to have its direct dependence upon the breath, and is like waves of sound wholly controllable by the muscles that control the breath. I can use it at will anywhere in the entire vocal range, and can increase or diminish the rapidity and volume of the sound-waves. It is easy to feel, when using it, that the breath is made to act upon the vocal chords quite as a violin bow does upon the strings—the *vibrato* answering to the effect of the player's left-hand fingers when set in rhythmical motion to make the throbbing sound string-players so delight in, and which seems to rescue the tone from lifelessness.

The vocal *vibrato* is quite distinct from the *tremolo*. Indeed, perhaps no singer is less in danger of acquiring the *tremolo* than the one whose voice has once gained the freedom which brings the *vibrato*, because the *tremolo* comes from a quite opposite cause—extreme tension of the muscles of the throat. Try to hold your arm perfectly still with the hand tightly clenched and the elbow bent so as to allow a hardening of all the forearm muscles, and you will feel it quiver from the tension. That is something like what the throat does to make the *tremolo.* String players use the *vibrato* quite as immoderately as singers do, yet how rarely they are criticised for it. Made by the facile fingers it easily degenerates, by mere rapidity, into a *tremolo,* which is not the case with the voice. To either executant it is so fascinating an ornament, that it is not strange to find it too constantly employed. I have often asked violinists and violoncellists why they use it so much. Some have so long done it as a matter of course that its use was habitual and unconscious, and they were rather surprised to note that their fingers were constantly in vibration upon the strings. Others said : " It makes the tone carry."

Voilà ! It is exactly the same with singers. The *vibrato* and *tremolo* are both the more or less conscious efforts of the singer to give the voice greater force, by sending one sound-wave after another in differing degrees of rapidity, as if to reinforce it with insistent, far-reaching beats. But the *tremolo* is a vice or a vocal illness, while the *vibrato* is an ornament too often used to excess. It is the pulse of the voice —the evidence of its vitality. To carry the figure further, the *tremolo* might be described as an abnormal, feverish pulse.   Fever consumes—means death.

I wrote you in a former letter about the need of uniting the head register of the higher voices—male and female—with the medium tones, and referred to the region, , as one of uncertainty—one in which it is a common mistake to force a broad tone upwards.   To some small extent you have been one of the victims of such treatment.   Now that you are freed from the necessity of so much public singing every week, and have not to temporize with the difficulty, and have had a period of vocal repose, you should try carefully a curative process.   Of course, no one ever yet taught himself to sing—trained his own voice.   As well might a tree be expected to prune itself. But some of the special treatment, applied for special needs, may be managed by the student alone.

In your own case try this, for a few minutes at a time, whenever your general strength is at its best: Starting with the *G* above the lines, sustain successive semitones downwards, each one with a separate breath and as long as that breath lasts comfortably—not to exhaustion. The two main things to remember constantly will be, that the same direction of the tone must be felt all the way, and the breath-pressure must be kept steady. Make a moderate swell upon each semitone, but in doing it be sure not to let the voice lose its concentration. By opening the mouth smilingly, so that the teeth almost meet, you will be most likely to feel the tone directed to the hard palate and acquire its purest, solidest texture. When you are thoroughly accustomed to the sensation of directing the tone so that it seems to deflect downwards and outwards from the roof of the mouth, practise accompanying the swell with a mechanical opening and closing of the mouth, so that the emission of the tone is controlled as it is in an organ, by the mechanical opening and closing of the lattice-work enveloping the pipes of its most expressive division—the "swell-organ."

The perception of directing the tone can also be utilised in the study of the *messa di voce*. In the first place consider the Italian phrase *messa di voce*, translated thus, "putting forth the voice," but remember that

it also implies "drawing back the voice."
Now take any tone that can be attacked
smilingly, with pure head voice—for instance
. Begin it very softly with the
vowel-sound "ah" as nearly as
you can get it with the teeth almost together. Do not be over-particular about
the vowel, but get the tone, although quite
pianissimo, very round. Be sure to press
with the breath by drawing in steadily at
the waist at the instant the tone is begun.
Then by continual pressure and opening the
mouth, swell the tone to the fullest point attained with ease, and do not at first be long
in reaching that climax of power. Up to
that climax is the "putting forth" of the
voice. Having reached it, draw the tone
back by diminishing the power, gradually
closing the mouth to its former smiling position, and pressing firmly with the breath
until the *pianissimo* is regained. In making
the *diminuendo* try to feel that you not only
draw the tone back into yourself, but that
you also press it down against the breath.

In your first attempts you will forget the
smile, and in remembering that you will forget the breath-pressure, but continual practice

will enable you to remember all the mechanical details and give more and more attention
to acquiring and clarifying the mental sen-
sations of tone - direction. It is extremely
difficult to write a formula for so subtle a
process, but it seems to me I could have
learned to do it to some beneficial extent by
reading a description of it. Anyway, try it
carefully and tell me what comes of it.

One thing more about breathing I wish to
add before closing my letter, and the difficulty is to find words sufficiently clear and
strong to express the conviction which is
mine from observation and from my own
personal experience. Here is the best I can
do now : Breathing controlled by the intercostal and abdominal muscles is of the highest importance, but do not let it escape you
that the unfailing *consciousness* of it is no
less important. While singing remember to
rely upon the action of those strong muscles.
Direct there a large part of the mental effort
whenever you sing. So you will divert that
effort from the operations going on in the
throat, and will gradually come to a feeling
of certainty in the emission and sustaining of
the voice.

167

LETTER XI

LETTER XI

Florence, October, 188–.

A S I get into the last quarter of the year's round and learn what each season is like, it seems as though each month's beauties were more fascinating than those of its predecessors. The autumn is not as ours—compensation for the brevity of summer. One would look in vain here for the subtle atmospheric effects which help to make up the exquisite loveliness of our autumn and our Indian summer, as well as for the rush of gorgeousness for that brief space when, with us, the woods

are aflame with tints which defy the painter's skill and resources to reproduce upon
his canvas. Here the heat of the sun remains to such a degree of ardour that only
yesterday afternoon I was fain to have an
hour's refuge from it in the dim, cool
spaces of the Cathedral. In them there is
always a sense of repose. Of quiet there
seems never any that is absolute, so clearly
is heard there the shuffling of a foot upon
the inlaid marbles of the pavement, or the
droning voice of the beggar whenever a
door is opened.

Yesterday, as often, there was a mass
going on under the dome, in the octagonal
choir behind which is placed the unfinished
"Pietà" of Michelangelo. The voices of
priests and acolytes reverberated noisily and
sent such confusing echoes about, that the
canticles sounded like an irreverent, unmean-
ing gabble. One seldom hears any music in
an Italian church—not even the organ,—and
these voices were truly horrible. When the
canticle changed the effect was excruci-
ating. Two acolytes turned the leaves of
the great book from which all sang, and it
was lighted from without by a lamp so

shaded that the rays were thrown upon the pages, and seemingly from within by quaint old "illuminations" done in colours and gold—many of them perhaps from the hand of Fra Angelico, who worked for art and religion—never for money. It amuses the "painter-boys" to know that his pictures in the Uffizi Palace are my first and abiding loves there; and, surely enough, when they questioned me about their drawing, "composition," etc., I found I had taken not the lightest note of such matters.

The pictures are to me the most splendid religious ecstasies, and to have one of them always near me would be to live in a Holy Presence. The gentle, pious monk of San Marco may perhaps now represent a mere "phase of development" (that is, something like the expression the learned ones use); but do you not think the artist must be known and judged by his power to compel the soul to recognize — not him, but itself? Some day I will sit down before one of those tabernacle pictures in the Uffizi Palace, and, with pencil in hand, will try to tell you better what I mean—a difficult thing to do always when one's farthest and finest fibres are stirred. It is to me a curious certainty that, if you could once lay eyes upon them, no words would be needed between us. Fra Angelico must surely have been one of those of whom it might have been predicted : " He shall see of the travail of his soul, and shall be satis-fied." Whatever of suffering he knew—bodily pain or anguish of spirit—must have been forgotten in visions of heaven itself before he could paint these happy raptures. And they hold within them the very spirit of music.

Late in the afternoon, as the day grows cooler, and the shadows of the tall houses cover the streets, is generally the time to cease my work for the day, and go out for a refreshing walk. Lately I found my rambles had left me, as they often do, standing be-fore Giotto's Tower. Why not ascend it and witness the sunset from its top? Noth-ing simpler if one possesses half a franc, good wind and legs, and a few *soldi* for the guide who must go up to unlock the doors. Lungs and legs felt fit for the test, and the *quattrini* were ready. Four hundred and fif-teen steps ! Wide stairways and narrow stair-

ways, lighted stairways, dim stairways, and
stairways almost pitch-dark! While going
up them the hour was struck on the great
bell above, bringing to the ear no clash—
only a rich, smooth, pervading vibration, just
as pleasant to hear as if it were miles away.

From the highest windows of the tower—
those long ones, lightly divided by the
lovely, twisted columns—one looks out as
from some fairy perch. The great height of
the windows and their elevation from the
ground give the eye free command of sky,
horizon, and the great city below. More
dark flights of stairs and the very top is
gained, whence one sees what he must always remember if he has a soul and a memory. How subtly must Satan have thought
out his scheme of temptation when he be-
guiled the Sinless One to the top of a high
mountain and then showed Him "all the
kingdoms of this world!" Any lesser being
would have dropped lifeless at the sight,
and this look over Tuscany fairly took away
my breath for some moments. Innumerable
roofs of dark-red, domes, towers, spires, bat-
tlements, gardens, groves, *piazze*, walls—
then villages, farms, castles, wooded hills,

valleys, the silvery curves of the Arno, mountains—oh! it was bewildering in its magnificent compass, its endless succession of beauties. It was thrilling to think of those who had seen it all from there, and upon whose haunts and works one looks even now. The kingly swell of Brunelleschi's dome is close by, and from the street I had never realized the loveliness of the lantern which crowns it. Down there, in the *piazza*, Dante was wont to sit where he could look up at it. No use to particularize, but far and near are churches, palaces, statues, loggias, bridges, which bring back great names—great days—great deeds!

Looking down to the space between the Baptistery and the Cathedral, it was curious to watch the passing vehicles and animals and people. Horses were like flies on the pavement, and the omnibuses and carriages were toys. Most amusing were the people passing close to the base of the tower, almost directly underneath me. They were just spots that moved about. One boy began to run, and the motion of arms and legs which suddenly began to gyrate about the spot was very funny. A monk looked exactly like a piece of black cloth that held itself up and concealed some apparatus that gave it a floppy, ridiculous progress across the *piazza*.

We are blessed just now with the presence in Florence of three opera troupes, but alas! it is quantity we have—not quality! The best of the three is a company playing only light pieces, and I heard recently a really all-round good performance of the " Cloches de Corneville." "La Fille de Mme. Angot" was also quite well done—and an operetta called " La Befana," not so well. At another house "La Sonnambula" is being given nightly. I have been twice. By constant repetition, of course, the piece goes smoothly, but it is marred by the badness of the Elvino. No tenor can make that mawkish part dramatically interesting— therefore all the more need of a good lyric artist in it. The soprano is excellent—one of those neat *voci bianche* (white voices) which Mme. M—— turns out by the score. Her Italian has evidently not been acquired in Italy. There was a smile all over the house when she sang something about her " *agnello* " (lamb) ; she meant " *anello* " (ring).

At the Pagliano there are heavy operas on, and I have been twice to "Les Huguenots" and once to "La Favorita." For the first the company was not sufficiently rich in good artists, though the Valentine was really splendid—one of the best artists in Italy,—and she worked the part up to a very thrilling climax, despite the fact that she was handicapped by having to work with a Raoul whose very good voice would not warm up to the work.

"La Favorita" is one of those operas in which a mediocre Italian company fairly revel. They enjoy it and let themselves loose in it with an excited energy which is sure to carry the house through a performance full of crudities and blemishes. In this instance we had for a prima donna a singer who has long been a favorite in such parts as that of Donizetti's hapless Leonora. Her voice was *passée*, and she looked old, poor woman! but her good will, and the determination with which she went about the business of the rôle were refreshing.

I do like those fine old-stagers who answer so to an old battle-cry! When the orchestra summoned this portly dame to the scene one could be sure she was there to work and win, if enthusiasm and boundless physical strength could atone for vocal freshness gone in the train of youth and beauty. When that immense arm launched itself forth in gesture, a big tone was sure to accompany it. From the first plunge she took us all with her in a mighty after-current. She made the orchestra give her big waves of sound, and upon them she rode securely. She carried everything with her rampant energy—Fernando, Alfonso, Baldassare, ladies of the court, soldiers, monks—all! They nearly all sang badly, but she roused them to a performance vigorous and picturesque. The colours were somewhat tawdry and crude, and plastered on with wholesale trowelling, but there was " go " in it.

When next you write be sure to tell me how you get along with your singing. The throat is better—quite over the old weakness, you think. Do not try it with much high music. Get the middle voice as easy and fluent as possible. You have your particular troubles, of course, but many a successful artist would envy you the extent and quality of your voice and some of the things you can do with it. Write me as fully as possible what your hindrances are in practice, and perhaps I can suggest some help. Signor Cortesi wishes me to tell you that the trouble with the downward scale probably comes from your letting go your hold upon the breath.

Speaking of your type of voice, reminds me to tell you that I have never heard over here a *soprano leggiero* equal to our much-lamented Marie L——. Two years after we were both in concerts with her, I sang with her again, and was astonished at the development of her vocal resources. That matchless organ, while retaining its lightness and agility, and losing nothing of its wonderful extent, had gained greatly in richness of tone and variety of colour. You would not have believed that a voice capable of such daring flights of execution as hers could accomplish with certainty and apparent ease, could ever attain to a style of such passionate breadth. It did, however, and hence the greater regret that the voice belonging to so pure and beautiful a nature should now be hushed in death. But mute as it is to our ears, it must surely live somewhere.

Nothing so perfect can have been perfected merely to perish. Absolute beauty must live on somewhere, conserved by its creator for high uses. And so if there is truly a heavenly choir whose music we wake from our last sleep to hear, Marie L—— must be one of its fairest singing angels.

I recently attended a most notable concert here in the Teatro Pagliano. It was given by an orchestra and a quartette of vocalists from Bayreuth, and the programme was entirely made up of selections from Wagner's " Parsifal." I cannot describe to you the devotion, the almost religious fervour, with which the crowded audience listened to that marvellous, soul-compelling music. By " music " I mean the numbers given by the superb band—the vocal parts being extremely unpleasing, and most of whatever dramatic impressiveness they might otherwise have had was lost by reason of their disconnection from scene and action. Putting them out of consideration, one felt as if, sitting there in the dimly - lighted theatre and hearing the great master's swansong, was something akin to assisting at a sacrament.

One of the painters, R——, was there with me. He is a German of Germans in his love for German music, besides being of German parentage, and he declared that no audience could have more worthily received that music than did those dark, eager-faced Italians. They applauded with sincerity and discrimination, and their attention was rapt and reverent all through the evening. I was proud of the quickness and the depth of their appreciation for the noblest music of the " advanced " school, and rejoiced in such fresh proof that they are a deeply musical people, sincerely catholic in their taste.

In no land is Wagner so lamented as in Italy. To her people he is the great god Pan of modern music, but his limitations are recognised by them. They hold that the human voice is the first and finest and most precious of all instruments. In the matter of developing the orchestra and writing for it scores which gave us new tonal values and colours, he was a miracle-worker. His conception of the general musical treatment suited to a great tragic story was always noble and vigorous. His grip upon stupendous themes was titanic. But considering him more particularly as a writer for the voice, it is my belief that we may rest upon a truism—that nothing in art can stand as a finality which is destructive to the organism employed in its interpretation.

Wagner wrote exactly what he felt must be said—not what he knew the voice could endure to say. I do not say that he could not write for singers, but that latterly he would not. More grateful and delicious examples of vocal cantabile than Elizabeth's prayer in "Tannhäuser," or than Walther's songs in "Die Meistersinger," are scarcely to be found, and all baritones are profoundly thankful for the melting phrases of "*O, du mein holder Abendstern.*" Many more instances might be cited, but nearly all from his earlier works. In all his later writing he represented a certain tendency.

Another decade of life and work would perhaps have seen him at one of two sometime inevitable conclusions. Either he would have produced other "music-dramas," like this powerful, mystic "Parsifal," in which the stories would have been illustrated by even greater orchestral writing, and acted for the most part in dumb show by very great histrionic artists; or else he would have come back to the glad recognition that the singing voice was not made to be treated solely as an ordinary integral part of his musical forces. He would then have found it greater than all instruments, and worthy to be heard in its purity and beauty, and would have given it a dominant place in his scheme.

The statement regarding art which I just declared to be a self-evident truth, finds its application in the fact that much of the music of Wagner and his imitators is directly destructive to the singing voice. Examples would not be wanting to show that purity of tone and correctness of production are sacrificed first. Then the fine sense of style goes, and as the ear deteriorates it ceases to demand accuracy of intonation. It is not an uncommon thing to read in the reports of German operatic performances statements like the following: " Herr —— showed himself the great artist he always is, although he sang flat throughout the third act " ! ! Did the critic mean the man was a great actor? Certainly he could not be a great singer and sing false through an entire act of an opera. Few can possibly sing the music of this new German school and remain fine vocalists. At this " Parsifal " concert, when the four soloists rose and began to scream at each other, all the expression changed in the faces of the eager listeners. The voices were bad and the singing was worse, and of a truth there was little to sing. And the worst of all was to feel that those four people, who were " Wagnerian " artists of celebrity and in the prime of life, had some time been good vocalists.

Richard Wagner was a great genius, but let us hope soon to hear his partisans taking that temperate tone in discussing his works which does not at present distinguish all their utterances. By the use of it they will bring about greater justice to his memory and a more catholic love of his productions, than can be engendered by sweepingly claiming for him perfection in all the details of his achievements.

> " O brave poets, keep back nothing,
>   Nor mix falsehood with the whole ;
>   Look up Godward ; speak the truth in
>   Worthy song from earnest soul ;
>   Hold in high poetic duty
>   Truest Truth the fairest Beauty—
>   Pan, Pan is dead."

LETTER XII

LETTER XII

Florence, November, 188–.

JUST a little way across the Arno, near
the Carraia bridge, is a door in the
Via de' Serragli bearing an inscription
which tells the passer-by that within are held
the services of the American Union Church.
I have been playing the organ there of late,
while the temporary pastor was a very elo-
quent Dr. R——, from Philadelphia.   He
was one day asking me about my life in
Florence, my studies, and their object.

Upon learning that I might sing in theatres, he seemed at first rather grieved, and

189

then his fine face brightened and he said: "I will tell you a story." Thereupon, he told me the story, which you must have heard or read, and which I will not repeat, of the meeting of the famous preacher, Father Taylor, of Boston, and of Emerson, and of the old Methodist's remark after the talk: "Well, according to my theology, that man has got to go to hell. But," after a pause, "if he does, he will sweeten all the place!"

Now, aside from the implied compliment to me, which was strong and sincere as far as Dr. R——'s apparent intention in the relation of the quaint anecdote was concerned, it was good to hear such a tale of Christian charity. But back of all that, what a puritanical and unworthy estimate the narrator seems to have held concerning what the church itself—considered in the broadest sense—fostered from the beginning.

Liturgies have always held within themselves the germs of dramatic action. In old times the church was the very cradle of the drama—in those very old times when she was, much more than she is in her factional condition of to-day, the arbiter of men's daily lives and their guide to the life to come. History furnishes abundant evidence that after the last vestige of the Greek and Roman theatres was lost out of the world, the Christian Church elaborated and increased her dramatic exhibitions. Her memorial processions and ceremonies culminated in the Passion Play. The mediæval theatre was the veritable child of religion, and if now that offspring has grown up to some vicious courses, one need not go far afield to look for the cause. A child disowned, cast out from the protection and guidance of home and parentage, is not too likely to attain to purity and honour.

To-day it seems high time for the church to reclaim her own and to find in the wanderer the most powerful of allies. The wave of reaction has already set in, and the clearest-eyed are beginning to see in all the arts the true and potent servants of religion. Just suppose, for a moment, that the church decided to have nothing more to do with music. The inspiration to produce the loftiest and purest compositions would be gone, and she herself would be terribly crippled for lack of the service music has always rendered her. She knows better than to re-

nounce that one of her children, and the day
is coming when she will recognize her need
to be in love and sympathy with all. All
her priests and preachers need, with a high
and solemn necessity, to be actors. Let them
see in the drama an art of the noblest possibilities—one from which they may learn
dignity of utterance, pose, and gesture—one
they should cherish as the best and truest of
helpers. The church is bound by ancient
obligations to do what it can to reform and
purify the theatre, and in doing it she will find
that the theatre has now much to teach her.

One day recently I sat in the maestro's
studio listening to a dramatic soprano who
was "passing" the rôle of Leonora in "Il
Trovatore." It often happens that I find
these artists of celebrity who in some measure owe their training to Signor Cortesi.
Whenever they are *disponibile* or are engaged
in Florence, they come to rehearse with him
even the most familiar parts, in order to
correct bad habits or to revive forgotten
"points." This lady is a beautiful woman,
with a brilliant, sure voice, and it was to
me as good as many lessons to note how
earnestly she threw herself into the part of

Verdi's unhappy heroine, yet saved herself by singing lightly the high and florid passages, even while giving the tragic emphasis all through. I was quite swept into the full current of the play as the piano kept up the narrative of love, jealousy, and intrigue, while Leonora warbled her affection and declaimed her despair. I had an hour of charming misery, but aside from that poignant enjoyment one learns so much by studying side by side with artists.

The only serious fault to be found with this soprano was that she constantly used the *tremolo*, and that is a vice unfortunately common among singers of every nationality. Asking the maestro about it, he said that as a defect it could not be too heartily condemned. The most common cause of it is, he declares, the extravagant orchestral accompaniments over which the singer must endeavour to be heard by pushing the voice to the extreme limits of its power. What a pity it is that the composers of the so-called " advanced school " do not study more carefully the finest and subtlest of all the interpreters for which they write—the human voice !

The All-Arts drama is the most splendid *half*-truth of the century. It degrades and injures the noblest (and the most delicate) of the component forces it seeks to enlist. But it is the great and natural wave of protest and revolution which arose to confound and overwhelm an emasculated and artificial school, and its recession will soon see us still nearer to truth in operatic art. The day of absurd *libretti*, and of such meagre orchestral writing as is found in the operas of Donizetti, Bellini, Pacini, Mercadante, and in the earlier works of Verdi, is past, and a new sun has risen—with spots upon it! Will there not soon come forth a genius who will tell us that even so noble a thing as a great orchestra is not degraded when it fitly accompanies the voice, sustaining it and bearing it upward on soft wings into a realm of pure song? There is no denying that the voice and its capabilities and limitations have not been studied with sufficient care by most of the recent and living composers. They ignore its finer qualities, treat it as an instrument, demand of it abnormal power, force faults upon it, and hasten it to ruin and decay.

Already several students of differing degrees of talent and advancement have found their way to my rooms, high up in this thick-walled old *palazzo*, and we have an occasional evening when we turn ourselves loose upon the operas. Little F——, an Italian pianist of positive genius, with a shock of curly black hair and the most wonderful great dark eyes, often comes in, and when the keyboard is touched by his powerful fingers we are all electrified into doing our best. Last night, with T—— and a very good baritone, we had quite a wild time over the trio in the duel scene in "Faust." F—— is so inspiring and helpful that I have engaged him to come to me three times every week. I am now taking three lessons weekly, and he will come on the intervening days and help me with the rôles which I am studying. An *accompagnatore* who does that charges very little—perhaps two francs an hour,—and with his aid one is free to practise acting and can much more easily commit a part to memory, by associating each phrase with its corresponding pose and gesture.

Good old Scheggi comes here for my

acting lessons, and it is great joy to see the enthusiastic old gentleman improvise " properties " and personages. He catches up a sofa-cushion and makes operatic love to it, or comically envelops his portly form in a striped blanket to show me how a conspiring villain wears his mantle. My expectation of seeing and hearing him in one of his best rôles was lately fulfilled in the musty little Teatro della Loggia. The opera was Cimarosa's quaint "Matrimonio Segreto," and this dear old man of eighty years capered about in the most agile fashion and was the life of the piece. And he actually sang his rapid *buffo* music with mellowness of tone and surprising truth of intonation. Who besides an Italian could do that at such an age, and who else with aught but Italian training could do as well even in youth?

LETTER XIII

LETTER XIII

Florence, November, 188–.

I HAVE written you much of Signor Cortesi, and yet it appears to me you can
know little of him from my sketchy
letters. It is easy and pleasant to tell of his
great kindness—his ability even greater—
and of his patience. Of those attributes one
cannot speak too often or too highly to do
them justice, and my speaking is but the
weak echo of the praise his other pupils
give him. By the Italian government he is

also recognised and honored. I have quoted to you his title of "Cavaliere," which was bestowed upon him in 1869. With titles as numerous as they are in most European countries, where the fourteen children of a count are all counts or countesses, there is small distinction attached to them, but only for great merit or distinguished service does this government bestow a title, and such recognition as Signor Cortesi has obtained is worthy of note.

Of something else he is much prouder, and of that I have told you nothing as yet. It is his famous sister, Adelaida Cortesi, who was one of the greatest dramatic sopranos of her day. She was born in Milan, but was taught singing here in Florence, by Ferdinando Ceccarini, and in 1846 made her first appearance in one of the concerts of the Grand Ducal court. Although singing by the side of so great an artist as Mme. Barbieri-Nini, she made a brilliant success, and at once had numerous offers of engagements. The following year she sang at the Pergola Theatre here, in Donizetti's "Gemma di Vergy" and Bellini's "Norma," and a few months later sang the latter opera at La

Scala, in Milan, scoring a complete triumph and establishing her fame as a great dramatic singer.

At Venice, in the season of 1849–50, she was chosen by Pacini to impersonate the heroine in his tragic opera, " Medea." Then followed splendid successes in other cities, and in the autumn of 1850 she was called to St. Petersburg to sing the répertoire of the most famous prima donna of the time —Giulia Grisi—who had fallen ill, and was so successful that, but for having made contracts in Italy, she would have remained long in Russia. Returning from there she had a round of ovations in the principal Italian theatres, and then followed a tour in America, beginning in Mexico. In New York I have found her remembered as a grand tragic artist, and in Havana and South America she was idolized. In 1861 the desire to see again her family, especially her aged father, decided her to leave the Western world, and from Venezuela she returned to Florence, renouncing the fame and fortune her career was bringing her.

In consequence of the death of her husband, Giacomo Servadio, a distinguished capitalist, she was compelled not only to occupy herself with the education of her children, but to manage her estate, which she did with consummate ability, although the details of business management were not congenial to her artistic nature. She lives in her country home, the Villa di Montecchio, near Castiglione Fiorentino. I have read some accounts of her career, and as her name has long been to me a familiar one, it is interesting to learn how she was regarded in her own country. Her voice was one of great strength and beauty, and she seemed to have been perfect mistress of its resources. Besides that she is credited with being " noble and soulful in action." Do you wonder that Signor Cortesi is proud of her splendid record ? *

* And now this noble, useful life is ended. It is more than four years since Adelaïda Cortesi died. An April morning—the year so young, and she herself far from aged—was the time when her nearest and dearest ones gathered about her for the long farewell. Make the sum of it all now : a great artist voluntarily closing her brilliant career, the record of which is tarnished by none of the stains which too often sully the life-stories of singers—a woman too noble in nature to think of herself and her laurel-gathering when, through the splendid clangour of orchestras and the wild plaudits of

The stories of the opera-idols of the past are full of vivid interest to me, and it brings the personalities of those people much closer to live where they triumphed, to remember that the theatres one frequents here once re-echoed with their voices. Some are silent in death—if death can really silence anything so deserving of immortality as a noble voice. Others linger on the scene more or less prominently. Angelica Catalani, one of the most marvellous of bravura singers, died in her villa near Florence. Carolina Ungher, one of the great dramatic singers of the mid-century time, lived and died here. Marianna Barbieri-Nini, for whom important works were written, including Verdi's " I Due Foscari," was a Florentine famous for the grandeur of her voice and the fire of her singing. Marietta Piccolomini, who created an extraordinary sensation in the musical

crowds, came up to her ever-listening ear the clear, far call of Duty. Regnant in the histrionic scene, her greatness inspiring those about her, she was herself dominated by the soft song of love and home which was ever in her heart and could make itself heard so that to her all other music was mute. The greatness of Adelaida Cortesi should be remembered always as adding beauty to art and humanity.

world, is now the Marchesa Della Fargna, and lives in a handsome villa south of the city. All the money—amounting to about a million francs, which she received in her brief but brilliant career, was used in works of charity, and although the illustrious family of the Piccolomini, which has often adorned with its name the political and ecclesiastical history of Italy, objected vehemently to her adoption of a profession, they and all Italy are proud to own her now as an ornament to that profession, to her sex, and to the nation.

Mme. Albertini-Baucardé, a retired prima-donna who was famous in New York, the widow of the great tenor Baucardé, who was the creator of the part of Manrico in Verdi's "Il Trovatore," is teaching singing here. I have met one of her pupils who has already started upon a career which will, I trust, take her to America. She is Mlle. Clementine De Vere, and the brilliancy of her singing reminds me of our *diva*, Clara Louise Kellogg. Another famous singer gives lessons here in Florence, Mme. Carozzi-Zucchi. Carolina Aljamo, now Baronessa Fatta, also lives here in retirement.

Moriani, the great tenor who rivalled Rubini, was born here in 1808. Of him I think it was first used, that phrase, "tears in the voice," and it is related that those who heard him in "Lucia" could not restrain their own tears. The Spaniards called him "the tenor of beautiful death," so exquisite were both his singing and acting in death-scenes. Here died Tacchinardi, another famous tenor—the one who was so unprepossessing in face and figure that, when he appeared first in a Roman theatre, he was hissed. Fancy the nerve of the man! He called out: "You came to hear me—not to see me." They listened, and forgot the artist's ugliness, and even his pluck, in the revelation his magnificent singing afforded them.

Learning of those Florentine sovereigns of the singing world makes one long to compel other cities to give up their treasures of musical history. All of them that are great in size, wealth, or historic importance, are the dwelling-places of famous artists who have finished their public labours, and of those who no longer need work unremittingly. Many there are who live in well-earned

repose. Others—from choice or necessity—
toil on as teachers. What queens of the
old realm live in Paris! Mme. Viardot
Garcia, the singing Rachel of her time;
Mme. La Grange, great artist and now
great instructor; Mme. Alboni, of the
matchless contralto voice, and who is said
to sing now as well as ever; Carlotta Patti,
whose lameness kept her off the operatic
stage, where her patrician beauty would
have been in keeping with the wondrous
purity of her voice. One can but hint at
the numbers of such celebrities in Paris.

Of London it does not do to tell tales, because no English singer ever really retires.
"Farewells" and "last appearances" he
or she may have galore, but such is the devotion of the English public to its favorites
that they are almost compelled to go on
singing until—well, until their voices are
but echoes of their past glories. It is a very
good arrangement for keeping the artists'
exchequer in healthy condition, but it has
some exceedingly bad effects upon musical
art in general. The much-vaunted "loy-
alty" of the British public to its old-timers
is all very well and has a most comfortable

and virtuous sound when the "British ma-
tron" quotes it proudly as a national characteristic, but it too often has the effect of doing
sad mischief by making people, who cannot
judge independently, believe bad is good,
black white, and wrong right.

The gloom of the London climate—
healthy as that climate really is—makes the
great city comparatively unattractive as a
residence for retired foreign artists, but it is
the home of a few notable ones. First
among them is Mme. Louise Liebhart, who
was long the idol of the opera-loving Viennese public. She was one of the first
really fine artists I can remember hearing,
and certainly her singing was of incom-
parable beauty and finish. It was when she
was in America on tour with Rubinstein
and Wieniawski—and with all deference and
respect to the Titan of the pianoforte, it has
always seemed to me that it should have been
Wieniawski and Rubinstein, for the Polish
violinist was in his line the one absolutely
great artist it has been my good fortune to
hear. Ever since hearing him it has seemed
to me almost a sacrilege to make the violin
anything less than tragic. The players who

treat the noble instrument as if it were a sort of *voce bianca*, with which to do things of astounding facility, have little to say to me. Excuse the digression. I was speaking of Mme. Liebhart, and wanted to add that that heroine of more than one hundred operas, with her pure style of singing, must be a most able *maestra di canto*.

In New York much of interest in musical annals might be found, but as in London, not largely belonging to the remote past. It is the home of many famous artists who wearied early in life of the arduous career of professional singing. Our adorable contralto, Annie Louise Cary, became Mrs. Raymond and retired just when reaching the zenith of her fame. Devoted to her domestic and social duties, she still finds time to be a helpful friend to young and struggling artists. Mr. and Mrs. William Courtney, both singers of great natural gifts, and, by the way, both trained here in Florence, early found their enthusiasm for teaching greater than for public singing, and many are the artists who owe to them the education that has brought success. Mr. Courtney has at his fingers' ends, so to speak, the best traditions of English ballad and oratorio singing, while few teachers in any country possess the thoughtful, analytical mind of his wife, Mrs. Louise Gage Courtney ; and you must be sure to read carefully her well-written little book called " Hints About my Singing Method."

In New York also dwells another teacher who was a prima-donna soprano of much fame, Mme. Cora de Wilhorst, now the Countess de Raucourt. She is a beautiful little woman, and though at the age when less gifted women cease to think of singing, often astonishes her friends by displaying in private a voice nearly as brilliant, powerful, and agile as ever. She is a lady of noble character, highly-bred and accomplished. There is no need to remind you of Signor Tamaro, the once celebrated Spanish tenor, for you have yourself profited by his able instruction. Signor Ferranti, who was the acknowledged successor of Ronconi in *buffo* rôles, also gives singing lessons in New York. Dining with him once at Roversi's, he lamented to me that he could not speak much English, and added by way of apology : " *Ma non sono stato in questo paese che venti anni !* " " But I have been in this country only twenty years ! " He still hoped to learn English !

Still another is Miss M. Louise Segur, a dramatic soprano who studied nine years with famous masters—the last three with Sangiovanni, in Milan. She now devotes herself to teaching and does thorough work. In fact I speak to you herein of few but those whose achievements I know by careful observation.

Clara Louise Kellogg, whose name is a household word in America, not content with the fine operatic career which gave her just claim to be considered the very first of American sopranos, leaves her home in New York for occasional and far flights over the States with her own concert company. Her pure, powerful voice, her great beauty, and her earnestness as an artist, make her welcome everywhere. Many a beginner may well learn lessons of patience and industry from the history of the triumphs this singer has achieved since in New York she first essayed the rôle of Gilda in " Rigoletto." In Europe she has been too little known, though her oratorio singing at

the Crystal Palace in London, a few years
since, gave her much fame there—especially
for her rendering of "*Let the Bright Sera-
phim*," in which the brilliant *timbre* of her
voice loses nothing displayed with the trum-
pet obbligato.

In speaking of singers of Florentine birth,
or education, or residence, I want also to
tell you that the Royal Musical Institute of
Florence, in which Signor Cortesi is *maestro di canto*, has given to the world many
fine artists, but only one of them is, I believe, known in the United States, and that
one is Signora Eva Tetrazzini-Campanini,
a soprano with a beautiful voice and excellent school. She is the wife of Cleofante
Campanini, the orchestral conductor, and is
therefore the sister-in-law of Italo Campanini, the well-known tenor.

The school prides itself also upon having
prepared for her career Maddalena Mariani-
Masi, a splendid soprano for whom Pon-
chielli wrote the music of "La Gioconda,"
but in its execution she has had a powerful
rival in our American dramatic soprano,
Mme. Maria Durand, whose career has, unfortunately for the land of her birth, thus

far been entirely abroad. For several successive seasons she has been the especial delight of the exacting public at St. Petersburg. Most of the American sopranos are of the lighter type, and perhaps Mme. Durand is our only operatic exponent of the grand style. Her voice is a true *soprano sfogato*—broad, powerful, and extensive. She is always a student—as all great artists must be—never content with herself.

Reverting to the school, Antonio Baldelli, who is perhaps the most successful *basso comico* of these days, is also an alumnus of the Royal Institute. He lives at Madrid, but his fame is over all Europe. Then there are Augusto Brogi, one of the leading baritones of Italy, and Giorgio Atrij, the basso — both from the same institution. Signor Atrij is celebrated as one of the finest exponents of Mephistopheles in Gounod's "Faust" known to the operatic world. There are many more who might be cited as doing credit to their musical alma mater.

But starting from here with this talk of artists, how far afield I have wandered ! I should have come back to Florence by way of Rome ! All roads lead thither, we are told, but we do not learn that they guide many great singers to a residence within the gates of the Eternal City. Perhaps painting and sculpture there overshadow in interest their sister art. But at least Rome has one veritable queen of song living there in tranquil and elegant retirement, after a reign whose glories are vividly remembered. She is now known as the Countess Gigliucci, but many would not recognise by that title the great English singer, Clara Novello. She was doubtless the most splendid exponent of the soprano solos in the " Messiah," " Elijah," " St. Paul," and other oratorios, that the British public have ever heard, and perhaps no singer will ever again, with such power as she did, pour into the very souls of a whole listening multitude the sublime and thrilling religious ecstasy of *" I Know that my Redeemer Liveth."*

And all these were trained in the Italian school of singing—the greater number of them in Italy itself. " What is the Italian school of singing," do you ask? The right school, and called " Italian " because the first great teachers were Italians. It is the method of naturalness. It is not lost because in these days of haste so few are found who will submit themselves to its slow, healthy, wise processes. When the fever for experiment shall have spent itself, we shall awaken from its delirium to remember that the students of all the arts have too much to learn by the old ways to waste time trying to invent new ones. What methods made all these singers so great? Those used by Italian masters from Porpora down to this day. Other nations have added nothing, excepting that the Germans, in leading the science of music to its highest present development, have created for singers a higher standard of general musical education.

There is no need of discussing French or German schools of singing. It would be quite as well to speak of Norwegian, Irish, or American methods. There are good teachers in all civilized lands, but being good teachers their debt to Italy is great, for here the Art of Song was born and cradled, grew to a noble maturity, and spread its power over all countries. There are no secrets about it—nothing to be lost out of the sum of the world's art-knowledge. Architects have not the ancient Greek build- ers' knowledge of how to construct great auditoriums of perfect acoustic qualities : sculptors may have yet to learn the true ideals of beauty by which Praxiteles worked, and painters may have to discover how Ra- phael of Urbino mixed his colours ; the world has forgotten how the Trojans made the iridescent glaze upon their commonest pot- tery, how the Tyrian dyes were manufact- ured, and with what cunning curves of belly and bridge the patient workers of Cremona fashioned violins until the vibrant wood imprisoned the first-cousin to a soul ; but for the patient student of singing no smallest part of the processes used to make the greatness of the first supreme singers is lost.

Charlatanism—the chicanery that is born of the breathless struggle for money—is the great danger. It exists in Italy and every- where else, but the student endowed with the requisite intelligence to work past medi- ocrity need not make many mistakes or be seriously victimized here. If he has char- acter enough to keep his soul free from poisonous greed for fame and wealth, his judgment and his patience can find for him all he needs to carry him on to the fulfilling of his lofty desire. Must not the teachers — considered in the broadest sense — be what the pupils demand them to be? They cannot make " bricks without straw."

LETTER XIV

LETTER XIV

The Royal Schools of Music in Italy.—Their Intended Influence upon Ecclesiastical Music; Upon
the Opera.—Desirability of such Institutions in
America.—Opera for the People.—What Might
and Should Be. — The Italian Poor and the
Theatre. — *Canti popolari.* — Hypercriticism. — A
Representation of " Aida."—The Stage-Carpenter
in the Dungeon Scene.

Florence, December, 188-.

IN a former letter I spoke of the schools of
music supported by the Italian Government, and have lately been learning
more about them and about many others
maintained by funds from various sources.
Besides the one in Florence, there are state
schools in Milan, Parma, Naples, Rome,
and Palermo, although I believe the Roman
school has assistance from the city and prov-
ince, in addition to that given it by the general government. Pesaro has the excellent
institution supported by funds which Ros-

sini left for that purpose to the city of his birth. In Venice a school is maintained by a society organized with that object. Reggio (Emilia), Perugia, Lucca, Turin, and Genoa, have music-schools supported by the municipalities—that of the first-named city also having aid from private sources. Novara and Bergamo have academies the burden of whose maintenance is divided between the cities and the churches. But the most important school in all Italy for the attainment of broad musical scholarship is that of Bologna, which was founded by Napoleon I. It makes that historic and interesting town the Leipzig of Italy.

These institutions, and many of lesser note, begin anew to make their influence felt in all the branches of musical art, by holding high the standard of scientific attainment and by gradually awakening the public interest, which has been dormant while political questions of overwhelming import have absorbed the minds of the people. They have already compassed some improvement in sacred music, and much more is sadly needed. One rarely hears any good singing in Italian churches, and the greater part of the organ-playing is beneath contempt. If the schools do good work in that field only, their existence will be more than justified, and some of them have for their especial object the advancement of ecclesiastical music.

There should also be an elevated standard of general education in music for singers intending to make operatic careers. Too many young Italians, with fine natural voices, go unprepared upon the stage—having but little sense of style and small appreciation of music as a science. In many cases the voice is not schooled so as to endure constant and exacting work, and consequently ages early or gets completely broken. In a few instances they learn to sing well by imitating good artists, but thorough preliminary training is not the rule. To be sure, one may have years of good instruction and still have certain things to learn which can only be acquired before the public,—things gained only by experience on the stage—but that is no argument against careful preparation. The uneducated singers not only run the risk of doing themselves lasting injury by their lack of preparatory study, but they confuse

and lower the public taste by passing off as
worthy art the tricks by which they manage to keep upon the stage. The government, hampered by a thousand demands
upon its resources, is doing what it can. If
other and richer states did as well we should
soon have a bettered condition of all musical
matters.

Perhaps not for generations yet will the
different divisions of our government at
home—municipal, State, and federal—see the
moral utility of founding and supporting
schools of music, and of sustaining the opera ;
but the time will come. It will sometime
be conceded that such institutions are no
more to be regarded as money-making specu-
lations for companies and individuals to em-
bark in than are parks, picture-galleries, museums, and libraries. We are rich enough to
have all such institutions, to fill the land with
beauty and to create in the hearts of the
people a desire for the things which adorn
and ennoble life. Some of them we have—
enough to justify us in a large hope for the
future ; but there are too few endowed institutions where the arts can be studied by
people of limited means. A school of music,

sculpture, or painting, is with us—at least in the intention with which it is opened—almost as much of a money-making enterprise as a butcher's shop or a bakery, and the bread and meat offered therefrom to the hungry might almost as well be jewels of Golconda, so prohibitive are the prices demanded.

And what a pity it is that a fraction of the money wasted yearly, in nearly every large American city, upon mismanaged "ward-politics" cannot be used instead to give the people lyric drama at prices all could afford to pay. Theatres for that purpose need not be expensive structures, and should not, to be good for music, have costly upholsterings. The companies engaged should be "stock companies" capable, by reason of working constantly together, of high-class work in ensemble—not consisting of a few overpaid "stars" surrounded by cheap people. This ought to be and could be. Let us hope it will be.

To the Italian poor the theatre is so much! Many have so little that can be described by our dear English word, "home" —only some place within walls where they cook, eat, and sleep. The few spare sous may well go for seats up in the fourth or fifth tier of the theatre, where for some hours they have light, warmth, companionship, and music. It is a softening and refining education to them. It is the very core of many poor lives, but they cannot bid high for its possession.

How well they know all the operas of the ordinary répertoire—"Il Trovatore," "La Sonnambula," "Lucrezia Borgia," "I Puritani," "La Traviata," and many more. I have heard it claimed that it would be quite possible to go into a full theatre where the first-named of these was being performed, and make up from the audience half a dozen companies, any one of which — soloists, choristers, and all—could go upon the stage then and there and perform the opera perhaps quite as well as the troupe before them. Going out of the house between the acts, one is likely to hear the score or two of coachmen outside singing the choruses of the work being given. On the way home the other evening, after a performance of "Rigoletto," I heard "*La donna è mobile*" all the way—not whistled, or hummed wordless, nor even warbled in half voice, but sung out with heartiness and zest. The bright, crisp strain would be taken up here and there by whoever had just been hearing its brilliant mockery in the theatre over poor Gilda's corpse, until its fascinating rhythm seemed a part of the winter night's splendour. Now it would be a mellow young baritone voice singing tenderly, and at the next wide, moonlit *piazza* a rich, free, well-posed tenor voice, the possessor of which had probably never had a lesson in his life beyond the teaching gained by sitting up there at the top of the house, and hearing all the best artists known to the Italian stage. One scarcely ever hears bad voices or bad singing.

This music is not the loftiest in the world, but at least it and the *canti popolari* are not trashy. Those songs of the people—many of which have never been in type—are most fascinating, and always go with such style and swing! And how the young lads can sing them! I have stopped in the street, of an evening, and waited for them to go by, some of them playing guitars and mandolines—a little company of five or six young fellows going homeward from their work.

Many such times have I been astonished to
see beardless, boyish faces after hearing
voices so full, so mature in tone, and so perfectly placed. The lovely Tuscan songs
would sound out so resonant, so passionately
coloured, and phrased with actual elegance.

Italian audiences have a *naïveté* which is
charming. They can "make believe" like
veritable children. Our critics have much
to say, and with some justice, about the
absurdities and inconsistencies of Italian
opera, and to the matter-of-fact mind the
things they describe are abhorrent when they
are not amusing. It certainly does make a
comical mess of the story when Leonora,
after nearly dashing her brains out in despair
upon the painted cloth stones of the tower,
bows to the applauding audience, and running to the side of the stage, drags Manrico
forth to take his share of the public approval,
and then calmly—nay, smilingly—consigns
him to his dungeon again. And it is rather
maddening, when once you have seen Margarita's body lying lifeless upon the straw
pallet and her spirit carried to realms of light
by attendant angels, to have soul and clay
reunited to appear before the curtain in the

person of the prima donna with excited eyes
and dishevelled hair, and led forth between
an urbane Devil and an apologetic Faust.
But after all, I do not know that it is worse
than the impossible Wagnerian dragon with
a booming basso like

" A very tough worm in his little inside."

The beast's efforts to be appalling are so
very funny, and tragedy is always skating
on the thin ice which is likely to break and
take a cold plunge into farce.   Possibly it
would be best to cultivate a facile imagination like the Italian's, and not be disturbed
by the incursions of bathos into dramatic
realms.   He welcomes his favourites before
the curtain with a sense of relief at finding
them not really dead but very much alive,
and not greatly vexed at being summoned
forth from dressing-rooms and alluring pros-
pects of supper.

Not long ago I went to a representation
of " Aïda " — one of those characteristic
ones wherein the success is made by the
spontaneous aid which the audience gives to
the performers.   There seemed to be an
electric communication between the two,

with frequent coruscations taking place. When the curtain rose upon the last scene, one could feel the audience bracing itself to bear the delicious anguish of the duet. It began presently. Amneris, kneeling upon the stone that has sealed Rhadames in the crypt in which her own machinations have condemned him to be immured alive, was calling out her pathetic "*Ohimè! Ohimè!*" while the solemn Egyptian priests chanted their "*Immenso Ftha!*" and Aïda was just beginning the wonderful swan-song in which the souls of the two devoted lovers seem ascending to eternal bliss. Just then some man, a stage-carpenter perhaps, not wishing to lose a note of that superb finale, opened a door at the back of the dungeon, and in the full glare of the light thus let in stood there, cigar in mouth, hands in pockets, listening calmly, and, gazing past the ecstatic, dying *amanti*, at the audience, seemed to have no remotest idea of being considered an anachronism or intruder.

The great *pubblico* in front were not to be disturbed by such a trifle in their enjoyment of the music, and I, curiously enough, found myself in such sympathy with them that all objection to the comfortable stage-carpenter seemed trivial and hypercritical. What is the use? Why fret ourselves over the passing imperfections of the splendid things which shall carry us up out of self and the plodding daily round into a higher, purer place—a place whence we would bring down a passionate yearning to live better and be nobler.

LETTER XV

Vocal Agility.—"To Know how to Breathe is to Know how to Sing."—Honest Methods.—Progress in Leaps and Bounds.—The Master's Patience with Stupidity.—The Scena from "Don Carlos."— Salvini's Great Acting.—Stage-Managers *versus* Actors.—Grand Opera in a Little City.—"Il Trovatore."—Six High Cs.—Choosing Songs—Handel. —A soprano's Repertoire—Some Song Writers.

Florence, January, 188–.

MY study has been very enjoyable this month and progress has been made. We keep at work still upon some Rossini music, and I have had much pleasure and profit in studying the "Semiramide" in company with the Danish soprano of whom I once wrote you. It suits her brilliant voice, and we now make the great duet for Semiramide and Assur go very well. The maestro rewrites and expands for us all the cadenzas, and those, as well as the shakes in thirds, we both have ample flexibility for, so the work goes capitally. As music it is not especially interesting, but the use of it makes the voice feel so comfortable and secure in other things. I am sure the value of *agilità* can hardly be overestimated, if only for the command of the breath it affords the singer.

After all, to know how to breathe is almost to know how to sing. Signor Cortesi is as kind and patient as ever in my lessons, and in fact is the same with all his pupils. His methods are the perfection of simplicity and straightforwardness. There is no pretence of mystery in the processes by which he works—no scribbling of cabalistic exercises which are his own secret specifics for vocal ailments. It is simply work and careful criticism over and over, until perception and sensation are so allied that the student demands and obtains from himself right tone production.

And there seems to be no steady, daily progress. I go on in the dark for days—even as long a time as three weeks—without seeing any effect, and then suddenly find myself past a mile-post on the journey, far ahead of where I was when the period of what seemed a perfect standstill began. Other students say they experience the same thing, and after all it is just as with other processes of improvement—physical, mental, or spiritual; one must go on with the daily round, do the hours of treadmill routine, and live upon the faith that no honest effort goes unrewarded in the end. "Nature," Emerson says, "hates calculators; her methods are saltatory and impulsive." But in my case the daily labour is not drudgery, for my heart is in it, so there is every blame for me if I wait not patiently for results. No exercise is too simple to be interesting. My only real trouble is that all too soon the limits of my strength are reached. A few minutes of really trying singing—no matter with what ease and freedom the voice is produced—and I begin to have a feeling of exhaustion, and cannot control my breath. At such times, of course, the voice cannot keep its right quality or place, and the greater my gratitude to my good maestro for the patience with which he works for one so hampered and so unsatisfactory.

If he has two pupils with whom he is even more careful than with others, they are

myself and a harum-scarum young Italian
who has not ordinary gifts of voice or musical intelligence. But the fellow's father is
an old friend of Signor Cortesi, and wrote
an appealing letter, begging the maestro to
take an interest in his scapegrace and try to
win him from his wild ways by getting him
interested in singing. So this great master
is loyal friend as well, and puts in long
hours of work which would be maddening
to a musician of less conscience and possessing less of the " charity which suffereth
long "—; for the scamp will not study and
has only a hard, tuneless voice, yet must
forsooth be kept interested by having songs
to sing. It is the old problem of the silk
purse and the sow's ear, but complicated
by having thrown into it all the swinish
proclivities of stupidity and obstinacy. It
is a lesson in humility and patience to watch
this man to whom great artists owe their
success, tugging through the hour which is
so apparently a pearl thrown to the unap-
preciative animal just alluded to, and then
rising from the piano with no sign of weari-
ness or annoyance beyond the brief eclipse
of the light in his beautiful eyes.

It does me good to tell you of it just in the same breath with my repinings over my own small trials. You are my ever-patient listener, and when I thus formulate to you a grievance there is sure to be something suggested that cures the ill even as I write of it. And after all, if that poor boy has less intelligence and less voice than I have, he is not troubled with the bodily weakness which must make me often a sore trial to the teacher's patience.

But now to work! Open on the music-desk is a noble scena from Verdi's " Don Carlos,'' and it is to be prepared for to-morrow's lesson. It is to me the very finest of operatic excerpts, abounding with magnificent phrases for the voice, and having an accompaniment most justly written—with color and richness all through, yet with such simplicity of construction as leaves the vocal part always predominant. I intended putting it upon the programme of a concert soon to be given in the Sala Filarmonica, but found it could not be used without getting permission from the publishers and paying them a fee of twenty-five or thirty francs. Therefore I have chosen instead a

scena from Apolloni's opera, "L'Ebreo."
It is a thing of older fashion and not as
meritorious a composition, but has a simple,
telling recitative followed by a broad melody into which much passionate expression
may be crowded, and which is a great favourite with the Italian public.

T—— and myself are to sing, and we
join in a duet, probably the one from "I
Masnadieri." I shall be fearfully nervous
after so long a time away from the public,
and with everything about my singing so
changed. It makes one think how amateurs
must suffer from stage-fright—that is, really
good ones. The bad ones are the "fools
who rush in where," etc., and ignorance is
their protection from fear. For the better
sort one should have great charity, because
it is nearly always "first night" with them.
If I go two weeks without facing an audience
there is timidity to be conquered. Signor
Cortesi is pleased that I have the chance to
try myself here, and says the Sala Filarmonica
is a fine room to sing in. It is the only
concert hall of any note in Florence.

This month has brought me the memor-
able joy of hearing Tommaso Salvini four

times, in " Othello," " King Lear," " La Morte Civile," and " Francesca da Rimini." Words would fail me in attempting to describe this remarkable man. We speak of all other tragedians in whatever terms of praise we can command, and still there remains this supremely great actor, head and shoulders above them all. Without having seen all who are called great, one cannot help forming an estimate of their comparative abilities. We have one American who, for virility in conception and for physical force, is perhaps nearly Salvini's equal, and we have a greater one who would rank with the Italian in point of scholarship, breadth of experience, and knowledge of traditions, and who would surpass him in beauty of person ; but it would take those two combined with several more of other countries to make up the sum of all the qualities this tremendous man carries in himself alone.

To me by far the greatest of his gifts is that voice—noble, organ-like, in its breadth and profundity, yet sinuous, changeable— never monotonous. It has the rich blare of brass, the delicacy of flutes, and the mellow persuasiveness of strings. In " La

Morte Civile " (" Civil Death ") especially
did it make itself felt by running the whole
gamut of human emotion, while the man who
owned the wonderful instrument kept comparatively quiet in the background.   It is a
play done almost entirely by voice and face.
His Othello is a grand, magnificent, prince-
ly lover at first, and then, oh ! then such a
fearful, dominant, jealous savage !   It is too
great to hope for suitable companionship on
the stage.   An Othello like that appears to
have almost no *raison d'être*, because he
makes any Desdemona seem unworthy of his
splendid passion, and any Iago a contempt-
ible cat to be flung snarling out of a window.   Salvini's King Lear has been much
criticised, and it seemed to me I could feel
that there were only phases of the character
to which he felt sympathetic.   As a whole
it was a trifle—only a trifle—less sincere and
spontaneous than the other rôles.

A more inadequate support for an actor
could scarcely be imagined than that supplied for this brief season.   The theatre was
too small and its scenic provision meagre in
the extreme, while the company was terribly
poor.   Yet the whole served to set off Sal-

vini's greatness — not by contrast; that would be apparent anywhere. I believe if he played with a company formed from the greatest actors to be found in all the world, he would be the jewel only worthily set. No, I mean it shows the supremacy of the man's power over himself, when he can rise superior to surroundings so bad that they would annoy and hamper a smaller creature, and can in the face of such disabilities create the illusion for his listeners.

The actors one hears most of with us and in England, seem to be a race of sublimated stage-managers who dazzle us with a superb *mise-en-scène*, and by taking to themselves an environment complete and picturesque in every detail, can fit themselves into the studied scheme as its crown and climax. The question is, have they really the greatness of the man who, upon a stage small and bare, with scenery and company little better than none at all, can yet carry us with him into strange scenes—over centuries of time—make us forget where we are—allow us only hard-drawn breaths in accord with his strong agony—alternately thrill, hurt, and soothe us with the magic of his voice?

Well, as long as we cannot often have such absolute supremacy of the individual, by all means let us enjoy a perfect ensemble when it is provided—only, do not let us be cheated by it.

Another recent treat was a trip to Pescia, over in the mountains between Pistoia and Lucca. A small party of us went by rail to Pistoia, and there we secured a *carozza* like a small barouche and had a delightful drive in the crisp winter air through a lovely, wild country. We were going especially to hear Sani, the tenor, and after dining at a little hotel we proceeded to the theatre, finding it very bare and ugly, but spacious, of admirable acoustic qualities, and well filled by a picturesquely attired audience. Pescia—a town of twelve thousand inhabitants—was having a six weeks' season of grand opera, with excellent orchestra and chorus, and some very good artists. Think of that and remember that New York has a better company—when it has any, and a longer season —when it has any, and has three million people, including those in the adjacent cities, to draw upon for audiences!

Well, the opera that evening was the ever-

green veteran, "Il Trovatore," and, judging
by the enthusiasm with which it was received, you would have thought it was some
new work whose fame had reached these
good people; and that they were now on
the *qui vive* to enjoy its beauties for the first
time. Dear old "Trovatore!" How mer-
rily its very villanies went that night, and
how the company seemed to feel the audience urging them on to the most spirited
rendition conceivable. From Ferrando starting up the sleeping camp with his vigorous
"*All' erta! all' erta!*" to the Count's final
cry of horror and despair at finding himself
the murderer of his own brother—from beginning to end—the opera went with that
large swing, that thrilling, captivating enthusiasm which always is the result when
people of even fair capabilities are before an
audience ever ready to help on and reward
good work. Sani was a prime favourite,
and his Manrico was, vocally, a magnificent
performance. His bright, silvery voice was
never for an instant wearied, and its tone—
more pure and penetrating than powerful—
made itself easily heard over band, chorus,
and principals. The "*Di quella pira*" was

twice encored, so that he sang the high *C* with superb force and brilliancy six times, thrice in the solo, and as many times directly afterward with the male chorus—and just as well the last time as the first.

An interim in the writing of this has brought me news that the concert in the Sala Filarmonica is postponed until spring. It is just as well as far as I am concerned—more time for preparation. I did sing only lately at a large musicale given by some English people, but was especially requested to contribute to the programme something German, so selected Schumann's "*Die beiden Grenadiere.*" You know I always had a certain success with that, but in its English dress as the "*Two Grenadiers.*" It is really easier to sing in German, and I have committed the words to memory, but find it impossible to feel the song as much as in English. I remember one concert when, upon getting fairly launched into the powerful phrases of the "Marseillaise," my music dropped unnoticed from my hands. It may have looked affected enough, but it could not be helped. The song has always been a sort of *cheval de bataille* with me, and

244

partly because I could carry its declamatory phrases along with spirit when a pure cantabile would have been uncertain on account of my voice not being "placed." To know what to sing is most difficult; and the formation of a répertoire is a process needing careful guidance and good judgment. Of course it cannot be done at all until the voice is in condition, so that its resources and limitations are clearly to be recognized. A singer should know a great deal of music, and use only a comparatively small part thereof.

I cannot tell you how much I should like to sing Handel. Loving it always, it has had fresh attractions for me of late, though there is neither time nor strength to do more than read over a little now and then. Nor is there teaching to be had in it here, because it is a realm unknown or unappreciated by Italians. They term it *la musica secca*— dry music ! Of course it has its formalism, but to me to sing Handel is to go back into the very spring-time of song—there is something so perfectly, imperishably, vernal about it. One needs to know much more than the three or four of Handel's oratorios which help make up the ordinary répertoire. There are gems in his forgotten operas—things for all kinds of voices, culled from works written too hastily or when the great composer was overworked and written dry. England is the home of that music, and when I get there much of it will I hear and study.

This Italian study is the best preparation for any vocalist's career, but woe to him who would rest content to know nothing more than the Italian operas! His aim is even lower than he knows, and the place where his education stops wholly and with no hope of continuance is close at hand. I wish it were possible to tell all singers and students of singing that they must not be content to be merely singers. Oh! if they would but see how necessary it is to be musicians—scholars — artists. With singers that last term has come to be merely a synonym for the word "professional." Some one asks, "Are you a professional?" and the answer comes, "Oh, yes! I am an artist." Is it uncharitable in me to see concealment or affectation in some students who tell you their aim is only a modest one—to sing in church or in drawing-rooms. Surely a larger aim is nothing to be ashámed of, and no one with a really slight ambition is likely to exceed the task he sets for himself. My best and wisest mentor in those things said to me long ago : " My son, set your mark high and never reach it, rather than place it low and never go over it." But you understand, and you feel as I do, so there is no need of saying more.

In speaking just now of the difficulty of selecting a suitable répertoire, it was in my mind to ask you what you are using mostly in these days. You are beyond the fireworks stage, yet it does not do to put your voice upon really massive dramatic music, however much your impulse of expression may urge you to do so. A *soprano leggiero* would soon sacrifice all its freshness and charm if forced on to fill a big channel. Yet your voice is not in the least a *voce bianca ;* it has colour through all its range so varying as to make it a puzzling organ to train. Its flexibility is one of its best points, but not its end and aim. You want music which is vigorous with declamatory passages, without being tragic—things of delicacy and tenderness. Be sure you get and sing the "*Solvieg's*

Song," by Grieg, and make it a model for the selection of others. You know enough of the opera things to keep up for purposes of flexibility and style, but you do not find them useful on many programmes—especially without orchestra.

Ballads? Oh yes, as many as you can find good ones. Use them simply—making each one a vehicle for some single emotion —for simplicity and directness are the very life of the ballad. Put all the homesickness you can imagine into your soul, and crowd that into your voice on every note of the "*Old Folks at Home*," and people will never tire of it. Make the "*Last Rose of Summer*" redolent with a fine, tender feeling of desolation that shall moisten your own eyes as you sing it out to others. Mix a mocking-bird's brilliancy and a coquette's recklessness, and pour them over all the phrases of "*Within a mile of Edinboro' Town*," and you have a dish to be served many times over. But know your Schubert and Schumann in the German, and from them you will draw many wonderful things for constant use, and will also find food and drink for your hungering, thirsting musical soul.

Know all and sing a few. Then if you have
time they will guide you to Grieg, Brahms,
Jensen, Lassen, Kjerulf—oh ! do not let us
forget Rubinstein and Liszt, even though we
are not bent upon making an exhaustive
catalogue. Try Liszt's " *Lorelei.*" Your
pure, easy high tones should give it great
effect. How splendid is the setting of the
fourth stanza :—

> " *Sie kämmt es mit goldenem Kamme.*
> *Und singt ein Lied dabei :*
> *Das hat eine wundersame,*
> *Gewaltige Melodei.*"

There are lovely things by Carl Bohm—
lighter music, but very vocal—also some particularly exquisite compositions by Gustav
Ernest, a young German composer settled in
London. His gift is exceptional, and will
yet command wide attention. The fact
that his songs are written mainly to English
words reminds me of two other London
writers, Miss Macirone and Miss Mary Carmichael. The former is known in America
by her beautiful part-songs, and her fame
would be much increased if she would give
the world a book of memoirs, which would be

most valuable by reason of her intimate acquaintance with many of the greatest singers and musical scholars this century has known. You must have an album of Miss Carmichael's songs—so spirited, so graceful, so sincere they are. There are of course many writers in London besides those whose names are well known everywhere ; I speak here only of some of growing fame whose productions you should know and use. And since we are speaking of English songs, why not of American ? The best of them are written under the influence of German teaching. If you do not know them already, select those of Clayton Johns, of Chadwick, Whitney Coombs, Harry Rowe Shelley, Ethelbert Nevin, and others whose names do not occur to me now. All these do not publish too much, as do some of the best-known English writers.

LETTER XVI

LETTER XVI

Studying Satan.—A Baritone Bewitched.—Overwork.
—Vocal Improvement.—Blurred Scales Remedied.
—Right Direction of Tone.—The Teacher's Need
of Varied Powers of Expression.—The Age of
Waste.—A *tenore rovinato.*—The Trill.—How to
Attain It.—A New Music School.—Signori Sbolci,
Altrocchi, and Chiostri.—American and English
Voices.—Why More American Girls than English
Study in Italy.—The Evils of Haste and Dissipa-
tion.—Lack of Devotion to Study.

Florence, February, 188–.

ANOTHER illness to report, but this
time it was soon over, and left no
bad effects. I was possessed by a
devil! Yes, I was hard at work upon
Gounod's "Faust," learning the part of
Mephistopheles, and that imp pursued me
night and day—was my constant companion.
I could not put him behind me, nor in any
manner escape from him. Did I take a walk
to try and throw him off the track, lo! he

would whisk out of some mysterious, dim corner with his

" Sono qui !   Perchè tal sorpresa ?
La voce tua, da me fu intesa."

And there he would be—scarlet clad, plume in hat, velvet cloak on shoulder, wallet at his side—a *" bel cavaliere,"* but fiendish, malignant.   I met him on the Ponte Vecchio buying the casket of jewels to lay at Margarita's door, and he skulked away among the shrubberies of the Cascine, eluding the silly Marta, while his mocking laugh broke in upon the lovers' tender duet.   Was there a wandering minstrel with a guitar—he sang only a crazy, cunning serenade

" Tu che fai l'addormentata,
Perchè chiudi il cor ;
Caterina idolatrata,
A cotanto amor ?"

Seeking the silence and tranquillity of the cathedral to escape him, I was in worse case than before, for to every penitent kneeling there in the gloom he called in triumph :

" Rammenta i lieti di quando un angel l' ali
Covrivano il tuo cor."

while every grim battlemented palace I passed was a prison wherein my fiend clung to Faust and the unholy bargain, and was defied by the dying Margarita. In short, he had so dominated me that I could get no peace. He was my Old Man of the Sea. In trying to master him, he had turned upon me to rend and mock me. This went on for a week, and then I suddenly found it impossible to remember two consecutive lines of the part. By the time I had committed to memory

" *Sei possente risplendente,*"

I had quite forgotten

" *Dio dell' or, del mondo signor,*"

so thought to let study go and sleep off the curious flightiness of my brain.

Sleep! No such Lethe lapped me in its waters of oblivion. I could no more sleep than I could invest myself with my Devil's bat-wings and fly to America for rest. With wide eyes I lay all the night and all next day, telling the servant it was only fatigue and she was but to leave me quiet. Another night of strange fancies and sleeplessness, and a second day, but at dusk someone entered my room. R——'s kind face bent over me and for the moment dispelled all disturbing visions.

Then came my best of friends, Sandy, to sleep on the sofa and be near me, but first they brought Dr. B——, one of the best and kindest friends of Florentine students—to see me. I remember almost nothing of his visit, but it seems he gave me some medicine, told them I was close to a congestion of the brain, and directed them to humour my whims. Two days later Mrs. P—— came with a carriage and took me up to the Torre del Gallo, where for five days I had most angelic care from the dear people up there, and then was packed off to Viareggio to let the sea winds blow the last of the dizziness out of my head—which they did most effectually in less than a week—and I returned two days since quite cured. Mephistopheles may now " gang his ain gait ; " he troubles me no more.

Lessons go on steadily again, and my indefatigable maestro says the voice is distinctly better for the rest. Its volume and flexibility increase together, as should always be the case. A voice exercised only in cantabile singing is bound to grow larger, and in such development will grow stiff and unwieldy and need constant replacing. Mind, you do your scales every morning, when your strength is at its freshest. Please do not neglect it. I know your industry, and can only fear you may not have time, or may feel the work done too much in the dark. But sing upon full, deep breaths, taken as low in the body as possible, and when any sense of difficulty comes, think of the inward and upward pressure until you get used to knowing what that pressure can do for you. Make it carry your voice upwards in scales, and do not let a collapse of the breathing muscles take place when singing downward. If you do the tones will blur—run off the track, so to speak—and make false intervals. In sustained passages, make the voice " swim " on the breath.

All that you can do by yourself. The really difficult part of the work is to get and keep a consciousness of the right directing of the tone, and even the describing of it is an almost hopeless task—simple as the thing is in itself. The hidden rock upon which most teachers of singing shipwreck is in supposing that " open " and " closed " tones are very differently directed—that the first are sent out with a sensation of going forth on a level, while the others are felt to travel upward and deflect forward on a curve. Here, instead, is what I have learned : In all the range of the voice, in the lower or " open " tones, up through the higher, " closed," or " head " tones—whatever you like to call them—the resonance must be felt by the singer in the head, just as if the sound was first directed toward the eyes, and then deflected outwards. The only difference is that the head resonance is felt more and more as the singer goes higher and higher in the scale. " Sing out "—" open the voice "—are directions one constantly hears, and as indicating mere phases of vocal training they are legitimate ; but the opening process must be done under careful and intelligent guidance, and without ever losing that important sense of direction.

Were I to attempt giving all singers and students a hint for general use, it would be to tell them not to " sing out," but to im- agine two distinct processes—one the breath pressing upwards against the tone, and the other the tone pushing downwards upon the breath. Instead of quarrelling in such fancied collision, they seem to unite forces and produce pure, easily-sustained sounds. It is next to impossible to generalize, because of the difference in students—differences of experience and capacity, and temperamental differences. Those last form the greatest difficulty the teacher encounters—if he knows enough to be conscious of the fact. How often we find teachers with but one set of expressions—one nomenclature—one routine by which to reach all intelligences. Brains differ as well as voices. What one student understands readily may be Choctaw to another with quite as good mental capacity. An illustration that serves with one may fail with the next. Nothing seems to me so utterly futile as the writing of articles such as one encounters in the musical periodicals— long screeds about methods of teaching singing, and I am inclined to believe they are generally advertising schemes.

If you and I had not studied together and discussed our experiences as singers and teachers, so as to have arrived at some common ground, it might be a waste of time for us to write about methods. The best teacher I know in the world—and that is Francesco Cortesi—has the least to say about method. His plan seems to be to set the pupil in the right way and keep him there until he could hardly leave it if he tried. If a voice has only three tones that are rightly produced, those three he will exercise, and by the time they are set immovable in their sockets, as organ-pipes are set, others are ready to work upon, and so gradually the entire compass of the voice is in shape to use.

But with this age of hurry upon us—with all the students wild to enter the arena of public work, thirsting for money, or fame, or both—it is a marvel that there are any teachers of singing left in the world. They have no chance to form artists. Boys and girls of eighteen, nineteen, or twenty think three years is ample time for study, and expect to be on the stage at the end of that period. The teachers spend their time starting the fledglings or patching up singers who, by reason of insufficient study in the beginning, find themselves crippled and are compelled to return to school. There is now with my teacher a tenor who started on the stage very young and with insufficient equipment. His voice would not stand the strain, broke down, lost its highest notes, and now its owner is obliged to call himself a baritone, and sings with a nondescript voice — a *tenore rovinato* — ruined tenor. How can the maestro get any practice in artist-making in this era of mad hurry? There are now no Pastas to work seven years to acquire the trill.

By the way, how is your shake coming on? You must not despair. No one knows why it is almost spontaneous and natural in some voices, and so difficult for others. It is possible to all, and to you it is necessary. Sing the two tones calmly and slowly, very legato, and without accent—giving the two equal weight. Keep the breath pressing upon them so as to to make a *crescendo*, and that will make you sure that the breath is an active factor in the work. Do this within a moderate compass until each two tones have a groove in which to travel easily and smoothly, and the shake is then not far off.·

Have I told you that Signor Cortesi has recently been appointed *maestro di canto* in the Royal School of Music here? He is often consulted about the affairs of the government schools. Just now he is projecting the opening of a new school in conjunction with several other teachers. All of them have such large classes coming to their residences that they wish to have more central and convenient quarters, so they will probably take rooms in some well-placed house, receive their own pupils there, complete the staff of professors by adding teachers of piano, violin, theory, etc., and also afford pupils the advantage of ensemble playing and singing.

I wish the school were in existence now, but affairs are not yet quite shaped for its opening. It is sure to be successful and celebrated, because these two are such well-known masters that they will have no difficulty in securing the co-operation of the most capable teachers in other lines. The advantages to foreign students will be manifold. How well I remember the difficulty I had in getting any information which would enable me to calculate expenses, decide how to live here, etc. This institution will have a secretary to whom any one desiring to come to Florence for purposes of study may write and obtain all needed guidance, even securing rooms in advance. Young girls can be placed where they will have, at very moderate prices, homes in which to live safely and comfortably while studying, also finding proper chaperonage to theatres, galleries, museums, etc.

There was a school projected here recently, as a branch of a well-known American conservatory of music, which was destined to be also a home for women students. The scheme fell through, but this thoroughly Italian school and its adjuncts is a much better one. It will be just the thing for students of limited means, because a master who would have (for Italy) large prices for lessons given to pupils at their own residences, is better pleased to receive the same pupils in a studio for about half as much. Then there are the collateral advantages of a school, such as class-work of all kinds in which students of singing hear each other and learn by comparison, have opportunities to learn the concerted music of the operas they may be studying ; while students of instruments will find similar privileges in their respective lines of work. *

I have talked with some of the Florentine teachers about their foreign students of singing, and it is with much pride that I hear them all say they are ever on the watch for American students, who are almost sure to have bright, fresh, vigorous voices. There must be something about our stimulating climate which tends to produce such voices. Of English students not much is known here, because most of them go to Milan, but I believe the same vocal characteristics prevail with the male students, and they are generally better musicians than the American young men, because they are almost sure to have had early training as choir-boys.

Few English women come abroad to study. There is perhaps still too much caste feeling prevailing in England to encourage young women of the best blood and education to enter upon professional work as singers, and when that is overcome it is not considered

---

* At the time of publishing these letters the above-mentioned school has been some years in successful operation.

safe and right for an English girl to live in the isolation and independence which is permitted to her more "emancipated" American sister. There are things to be said on both sides of the question, and to me the so-called "independence" of our girls over here is often painful to see. But the fact remains that there are more American women than English who become famous singers, and it is evidently because an artistic career is considered desirable and honourable in our country, and therefore attracts our best born and best educated girls. When an Englishwoman of such origin and advantages does become an earnest professional singer, she is greater and goes farther because she has less of the feverish haste which is the curse of Americans. We produce many brilliant artists, but our Clara Novello is yet to be.

There is another evil besides hurry. It is dissipation, and it is noticeable among our girls as well as the young men, but in a different form. Do not be shocked; I am using the word broadly. A young woman who comes here to study singing should not be seen every afternoon about the galleries, churches, and museums, and before shop-windows—Baedeker in hand. It is her form of dissipation to fly about, see everything, go everywhere, get "culture"—and then go to her lesson with fagged mind and body. I have known of bright, gifted girls here who really never gave their teachers any chance to work upon their voices. I am the last one to decry the value of a many-sided education for an artist. No one more than a singer needs to store his mind with knowledge and fill his soul with beauty, but when the time comes to make the most of the voice, as a voice alone, the student should live for that and concentrate upon its development all his attention, and conserve for it all his strength.

As for those of the other sex—well, they are too often boys with little general musical preparation, and limited ideas of what equipment is needful for an artist. They get over here and feel at once the charm of the easy, Bohemian life, and finding themselves emancipated from the restraints of home, with no responsibilities to family or society, are led into a manner of loose living which is, to say the least, time-wasting.

They find it impossible to study much, and lay that to "the climate." Rarely do they acquire the language with any degree of thoroughness, and in many cases it is because they have little accurate knowledge of the grammatical construction of their own tongue, so as to be able to learn by making comparisons. They merely "pick up" the Italian, which generally means the acquiring of enough to talk of the weather or the theatre, and a few such every-day subjects—all with a viciously bad accent. The voices are generally good enough, but I am daily astonished at the lack of devotion to study, the amount of time and strength wasted by our students. The teachers nearly all complain of the evils—at least all those do who are themselves in earnest and anxious that their pupils should make progress.

LETTER XVII

LETTER XVII

Letter to a Baritone.—Who Should Study to Become Professional Singers.—Voice not the Only Quali- fication Necessary.—Bad Teaching.—Why Stu- dents Should Come to Italy.—Charlatanism in America.—The Dying Monk and His Legacy to a Fiddler.—Traditions.—Common Sense in Teach- ing.—What Happens to one who Delays.—Better than Bohemianism.

Florence, March, 188-.

I SEND you this time a copy of a letter just sent to an old friend who wrote to ask me about the advisability of his studying to be a professional singer and about coming here for such study. This letter includes some things I had in mind to say to you, and wherein it repeats what has already been said I would have the repeti- tions go for emphasis, therefore you shall have it *in toto*, as follows :

" MY DEAR L—

" It is a pleasant task to answer your let- ter of inquiry about the life and work of a student of singing here because you settle in it all the preliminaries, render excuses unnecessary, and really invite me to talk my beloved 'shop.' So let us be at once of the shop shoppy, and if what this contains shall decide you to come to Florence I shall rejoice to have been of use to you and to be here to welcome you. You ask me to write at length, replying to your questions in any discursive manner that comes easiest, and to touch upon the general advantages and drawbacks of professional study and life in Italy. It would be a ' large order ' from any one but a friend and a fellow-enthusiast. You are both in one most delightful personality, therefore it is, let me repeat, a pleasure.

" Yes, you are an enthusiast, but as yet you are undecided about undertaking the arduous career of a public singer. A musician you are and always will be. I have, in the course of a year, many letters from both acquaintances and strangers, asking my advice about entering the profession of singing. Always my answer is :—' Do *not* if you can help it.' You know what that means. Happy the few to whom such a question never occurs—those whose earliest memories are of song, and of knowing that to be a singer is for them the only possible aim and end of living ; not a question of talent or of choice—only the inborn knowledge of being chosen.

" With all those others who are only musically-inclined there comes, generally in early manhood or womanhood, a point when the possibilities of success in this profession must be considered and balanced against the difficulties of gaining entrance to it, of acquiring preparation for it, or against the chances of better results in other fields of labour. I cannot always clear my mind of a bit of resentment against such calculating spirits, although they do sometimes seem to achieve much when once they elect to enter the lists. To me art is a goddess who may choose her followers rather than stand in the market-place to be chosen. It irks me to have people speak as if in some manner they were honouring her by deciding to become artists, and such antagonism at the outset makes it almost impossible for me to advise them about ways and means.

" Too many such people dream that voice is the sole qualification of fitness for a career as a singer. It may well be the first, though doubts will arise as to even that admission when one remembers all the great artists who had defective voices to begin with. In some respects you do well to come with your questions to one who has had, and is still having, a regular pitched battle with vocal disqualifications, which, if they did not all exist in his natural voice, were imposed upon him by lack of guidance very early in life, or by wrong teaching later on—both terrible evils, because they double the work of the reconstructive process, making unlearning necessarily go on as the hampering companion, the Old Man of the Sea upon the weary shoulders of acquirement.

" I have lately learned—and not at all to my surprise—that when I first came here to Florence, some of the other students used to say, with a mixture of scorn and pity: ' Poor W—— ! He has no voice and had better have stayed at home to save his time and money.' Save my time and money ! What for ? What to do with them ? The criticism was a natural one if there is taken into the account the rather low standpoint of judgment of those who uttered it, and it would not embitter me even, if I had not already made more public appearances here than any of my critics, had more success, and shown greater progress in every direction. My voice had had done to it about all the mischief the teachers of the quasi-scientific school in America could compass, and added to the consequently chaotic condition in which it arrived here was the serious drawback of ill-health. What could be expected, especially as the voice is naturally a broad one and needs a sound physique to carry it?

" So much I need to tell you at first about myself, for the most you know of such vocal resources as I possess you learned from hearing me in light opera—a business which has little to do with art in any form, and especially little with vocal art. Is not that true? Now that I have been here more than a year you would see some progress and a great change, although it seems to me but a few months since I began to feel a really decided impetus carrying me onward. There was at first, as has been hinted, such *impedimenta* to throw overboard, such a clearing away of mentally hampering consciousness, before I could feel myself fairly afloat. Why! when I went to Signor Cortesi, my *maestro di canto*, he told me that nearly everything was wrong in my singing, that he could not predict the possibility of ever making a singer of me, but added that he had a curious conviction that there did exist something worth while, and that he would accept me as a pupil if I would work. Work? Well! one can work for one's salvation, be it spiritual or only vocal—and the two often seem but one! The difficulty is not to overwork.

" Now, summing up my experience and observation, it is possible for me to say to you what I stand ready to say to all earnest students of vocal art: As long as Italy is Italy, with her climate, her language, and her traditions, the best will come here to take what she has to give them from those resources. In this, as in any old civilization, the student can have the needful tranquillity for his work, the withdrawal from that feverish existence which is a poison we Americans, of all peoples, imbibe without always knowing it. In Italy, along with serene retirement, one secures a constant inflowing of subtle artistic sympathy which feeds and sustains one with more or less tangibility. Then the climate is certainly something like in effect to Silas Wegg's famous pasty— 'mellerin' to the organ!' The use of the Italian language, not only in singing but in conversation, with its simpler, ampler vowels, gives one a freedom of tonal emission not to be learned from English alone.

"Finally, as to what I have termed traditions—ah! that is difficult to explain. It does not mean that the Italian *maestri di canto* hold and conserve certain ancient secrets about the training of the voice. No, it is something far less definite than that, although the existence and possession of such secrets is a claim often set up by charlatans who profess to teach by 'the old Italian method.' In America they are to be counted by the score. Sometimes they are clever and unscrupulous young Italians who have picked up a little English to follow over here the business of *accompagnatori* to English and American students. It is their task, at from one to two francs per hour, to play over the operas for such students and assist them to learn a répertoire. In that way they get a

knowledge of 'points,' style, etc., and without knowing anything thorough about the
voice, they set up in English and American
cities as *maestri di canto !* Or they may be
the chorus directors of stranded opera companies in those countries. Often they are
only members of the orchestras of such companies. In one case I know of it was a fiddler who drew in scores of victims by pro-
claiming that an aged monk in Italy was the
last one surviving who knew these wonderful
secrets of vocal art, and that this *frate*, upon
his death-bed, had revealed them to him, so
that he—the out-of-employment fiddler of an
opera-troupe—was now the sole inheritor
and exponent of the veritable 'old Italian
method.'

"How beautiful ! How one is struck by
the wisdom of Providence, which decreed
that the art of training voices should not be
quite lost, but should trickle down precarious-
ly through yet another generation, carrying
in its beneficent flow some golden sands into
the pocket of the good old monk's fortunate
legatee !

"There are perhaps worse evils. Of all
people, my dear L——, beware of the man

who demonstrates to you from anatomical charts and from a human larynx pickled in a bottle of spirits, that when you attack the middle *C* your arytenoid cartilages must pull a little toward the southeast! None of that nonsense is heard in Italy. Until we can clearly observe all the workings of the throat and note every cause and effect, it is well to remember that ' a little knowledge is a dangerous thing.' A philosopher adds to the wholesome proverb this suggestive declaration : ' A falsehood is mischievous just in proportion to the amount of truth it contains.'

" Our method-cursed teachers (?) of singing work unlimited harm by getting hold of half-truths (we need not be particular about the fraction !) and constructing from them the Procrustean bed which each one dubs ' My Method '—with two big Ms ! They stumble upon some part of a truth that for ages has been known and used in its entirety by the real masters of singing. This moiety they claim as a discovery, and proceed to describe it in scientific terms and parade it as their own. Each one has some such doll to dandle and display, and takes the keenest pleasure in writing pamphlets and newspaper articles to ridicule his neighbour's pet puppet. They are all like petulant children ; one carefully sets his blocks up in a pretty row, while the others watch their chance maliciously to topple the first block and hope to have the delight of seeing the whole structure come clattering down. No, there is charlatanism everywhere, but not in Italy does it take 'that anatomical form in the teaching of singing.

"In America, our Land of Hurry, one can count by dozens the people who have discovered new and rapid processes. Each professor owns a sort of mill of his own invention—crude voices tumbled into one end and warranted to emerge from the other as the most highly-polished and marketable articles !

"But what about the traditions ? you ask. From time immemorial—it does not matter how or why, but very likely fostered by language and climate—Italy seems to have produced voices free and pure, unobstructed in their natural manner of emission. Perhaps the first few singers who came before the public in the churches, as wandering troubadours or *improvisatori*, or later on in the opera, chanced to be really good singers, and thenceforth served as models. It is said that in England the great tenors of the past, Incledon, Templeton, Braham, and others, were slightly throaty in their singing, and that as a consequence nearly all the tenors of to-day in that country have a tendency to throatiness, so that the general notion prevails that a voice must have a little of that quality to be truly a tenor.

"However that may be, it illustrates the subtle force of ideas perhaps transmitted to us from the pioneers of our profession, and it seems to me that the best Italian teachers have been so saturated with the right things in voice production, that they cannot allow their students to do the wrong things. They are able to say: 'This is right—that is wrong; do this—not that.' What need of more? I do not find that these *maestri di canto*, neither the ones I have had nor those who teach other students, have much 'method.' The subjects to be treated are too various, the means of treating them and the application of those means, too subtle to admit of the process of crystallization into clearly-defined progressive steps. What student can study by himself the published 'method' of any of the writers and make a singer of himself by its aid?

" In Italy the rule is the use of the good, old-fashioned, every-day, well-wearing article—common-sense! Given a good musician either a retired operatic artist, or a director of opera, or one who has made voice-training a study by much careful thought and by acquainting himself with the best vocal models, and let whichever it is be both conscientious and industrious, and then the process is to him somewhat as is to an experienced gardener the training of a tender shoot into a vigorous tree. The delicate stem must be bent this way a little and that way a trifle, in order later to relax into perfect straightness. Its growth must be equal and symmetrical in all parts—its branches carefully adjusted as they appear—its proper food supplied to give it a texture of combined firmness and flexibility. It is a slow process, and to me it sometimes seems as if in their gardening the Italian *maestri di canto* were slower than need be. At least it has seemed so, but lately it has dawned upon me that they are right, for with the voice it is just as much a matter of assimilation as of acquiring technique.

"Then there is the business of expense, and I know that you, like myself, have that to consider carefully. Suffice it for the present to say that I pay here in one month, for daily lessons, exactly what in New York I should give for five lessons, and that I live here and go to the opera freely for what would pay there about half the bare cost of living alone. In another letter I can, if you wish, give you all details concerning the prices for rooms, meals, hiring of piano, lessons in language—everything of the kind. But come if you can, and learn what can be done in study when one is withdrawn from other interests and is able to make it the first of all things, not something which is to be done as well as may be with the dregs of time and strength.

"You have made yourself a capital musician, so the foundation is laid, and you have a beautiful voice with which to work upward. Shall I predict what will happen if you delay long? You will fall in love with a woman, who must be, to capture you, both beautiful and good; you will marry her, and be thankful forever after that you did; there will be lovely children to cluster about your knees, and with bread to earn for all, you will be forced to give up personal ambition and will settle to the staid, respectacle life of a teacher. You will play the organ in a church, and tear your voice to shreds training a casual choir. And you will be happier so than you ever could be in the mere Bohemian life of a singer. It is quite possible that all the domestic happiness might come later, after you should have secured to yourself here what would always be a help and satisfaction to you, but I forbear to urge anything. You will do the right—no fear to the contrary—and it is not for me or any man to lay compelling hands upon destiny. *Che sarà sarà.*"

LETTER XVIII

LETTER XVIII

Florence, April, 188–.

TO be tried and not found wholly wanting is a relief and satisfaction after a period of close preparation for the ordeal. It was one of the last days of March when I stood before a large audience in the Sala Filarmonica and sang, besides some concerted music, a scena from Apolloni's tragic opera, "L'Ebreo." It was nervous work at first, after having been so long away from the public, and of course the feeling of singing is very different to me now. I had, so to speak, to get acquainted with myself, but being one of those who do not often show trepidation, I had not the discomfort of feeling that the audience was too much occupied in being sorry for me!

The recitative went tolerably and secured at its close a little encouraging applause. As soon as the broad, vigorous melody was started :

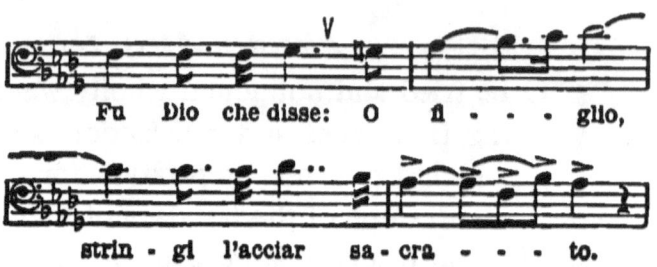

and I felt the swing of it, there was real pleasure in the sense of amplitude and certainty in the voice. At the end there was applause so cordial and prolonged that I returned to the stage to bow.

During the intermission several of the critics who represented the daily papers came into the green-room to say kind things to me, and all had one phrase of advice to utter : " *Bisogna cantar più francamente,*" and urged me to use the same selection at the next concert, so as to make the direct effort to deliver the voice more freely. This was done a few evenings later, and with a measure of success. At a third concert I sang a scena from " I Lombardi," which made me feel still more strongly the effect of study in reforming and increasing my voice.

The latest concert, and my last one in Florence, was given in a church and for a charity. Its chief patron was the Princess Mary Adelaide, Duchess of Teck, the handsome, big-hearted English princess who is cousin to the Queen of England, and who, of all the ladies of the royal family, is most the friend of artists. Her Royal Highness, accompanied by the Princess May and Prince Francis, was at the concert. Another patron was a Russian lady, the Princess——, and she was also one of the singers, her solo number being the Stradella prayer, "*Pietà, Signore*," which she sang with considerable beauty of voice and expression. My own selection was the "*Pro Peccatis*" from Rossini's "Stabat Mater."

How difficult it is to tell what you are doing when singing in a church where no demonstration from the audience is to be expected. In the concert-room one knows subtly whether he is reaching the sympathies of the listeners, knows it without waiting for applause to prove it; but in a place where plaudits may not be given an apathy seems to settle over the audience and stop the current of feeling that might otherwhere keep it in touch with the performer. Of course I speak of the effect of *pezzi staccati ;* a mass or an oratorio is, by means of the interest aroused and sustained by the story, generally sufficient to keep up some sympathetic communication with the hearers which gives more or less tangible help to the artists. I say more or less, because it is my belief that the amount and quality of the aid one gets in that silent manner depend mainly upon the temperament and the mood of the artist himself.

Upon this last occasion I sang with determination and spirit, but could not feel any satisfaction over the performance—perhaps in part because Rossini's " Stabat Mater " does not kindle me to the feeling which certainly is roused in one's spirit when the wonderful Latin hymn is wedded to truly religious music. You know what Richard Grant White said of the " *Cujus Animam* " —that it was " about as expressive of the sorrows of the Divine Mother as the leaps of a kangaroo would be ! " That is perhaps quite as grotesque as it is true, but it always seems to me that Rossini's music was just the creation of beauty for beauty's sake, and was not born of deep religious feeling.

Some days after the concert the Princess Mary Adelaide sent me word that she wished me to come and see her, and that she would soon send me an appointment for the visit ; but now I am on the very eve of de-- parture from Italy and have been obliged to say so to Her Royal Highness. It is quite like her to extend to an artist such spontane-ous kindness. In Florence, as elsewhere, she is beloved for her amiability and generosity. Perhaps later, in England, she will think of me and care to stretch out a helping hand.

Another outcome of these few public ap-pearances has also been very pleasant. Since making known my decision to go to Lon-don, some well-known Florentine musicians have sought me, here in my rooms and else-where, to urge me to remain in Italy for operatic work. Hearing me sing, or read-ing some notice, had been enough to make these warm-hearted Italian artists come to offer a hand-clasp and a kind word, and to seek to retain in their dear country the one their charity deemed worthy of her recognition.

But it must close now—the pleasant life here—and he who has written you these poor letters tells you now out of a full heart how wholly inadequate they have been to describe the worth and loveliness of all that has surrounded him in these rapidly-fleeting student days. It has been a generous, full-handed time, and if its opportunities have not all been used for the best, it is to be hoped they have not gone by forever. Possibly there is not much to show for the sixteen months which now seem the very core of life as I look back upon them, but within me is the certainty of an impetus gained—material acquired for future use and assimilation. Progress in any art, to be real, must be deep and many-sided, and can be measured by no yardstick nor sounded by line and plummet.

The farewells are all spoken—to friends, to fellow-students, and to my beloved maestro. The last, need I tell you, was hardest of all. It is not often given to anyone to find as faithful an instructor and as true a friend as Signor Cortesi has been to me.

Milan, May 1st.—Before going hence out of this dear, bright Italy, it is needful to try again to tell you what it has been to me, even though the attempt makes me feel that words are empty things—only better than silence. Yesterday, when the softly rounded hills among which the railway curved took Florence from my gaze, they also held in long eclipse all the beauty and joy of the spring. It was as if the day of life had reached its grey evening-time, and with the sense upon me of great and final loss, I could not, for many hours, remember to be glad and grateful for what was mine to carry away and to keep indelibly in heart and memory.

To-day there is no shadow; I speak to you out of abounding happiness. Of all the harassing interruptions in study you know the history, but not even you, who are closest to me in the tie of artist-sympathy, can know how sweet it is to begin here, in this fitting season, to nourish and cherish the good seed sown within me during the past months. It is my pleasant task to begin now to recall things learned and try to pass them before me in orderly review, with the hope of making them useful to myself and others. Of empirical knowledge in the realm of music there would perhaps be little that is new to put before you. It is true that I could sing operas to you, *da memoria*, for hours, and could tell you afresh of varied studio experiences, but those things seem to me now but emanations—like the scent of the brown earth which pervades the spring air and is but the proof of life and growth. The real, the lasting thing, is the plant itself, that which fructifies by and by.

If in my letters I have wearied you by lamenting my physical inability to do all the actual work required of a student, let me now plead that it seemed needful to speak of that drawback, not only to account for the time lost from study, not only to prevent your having unfulfilled expectations with regard to my achievement as a singer, and not only to stimulate you also to do your best through many discouragements, but to keep ever before my own consciousness that, inasmuch as I was lacking in exuberant bodily strength, it was all the more emphatically necessary to work mentally. The iteration of facts and circumstances which have been my hindrances here, has helped me as it may help other students similarly hampered. It has kept me ever mindful of the need of noting and analyzing the processes of study and of labelling results, and laying all away in memory to ponder over and utilize in the future. It has made me watchful to rescue from the current of daily life among students, artists, and masters some flotsam and jetsam for my storehouse.

And if I need other excuse, pray find it for me in the occasional floods of misery that have swept over me when, working upon some marvel of composition, weakness of body has prevented my coping with its exactions. The telling of the difficulty has often brought back to me the billow of hope upon which I could ride and rest while gaining strength for another few oar-strokes onward. Humanly speaking, I am content— not with myself, but with the turn in the road now at hand. There is no disappointment to put on the record of these days. I came to do whatever was possible, knowing the darkness of the future, ever recognizing the wisdom which denied its unveiling—but sure of light enough for each successive step. Could one ask for more ? Little by little— "from strength to strength." To feel that at least nearly one's best has been done, and to carry away from the scene of such striving the warm good wishes of friends whose friendship will not fail in absence, is—if not happiness—a fair measure of content to which abundant hope is added.

"Honest work for the day, honest hope for the morrow,
 Are these worth nothing more than the hand they make weary?"

Upon arriving in Milan it was vexatious to find La Scala closed. For a singer to come here and not attend at least one performance in the famous theatre is truly disappointing. However, it was easy to gain access to the building, and even to go upon the great stage and imagine what it would be like to face an audience from there. I sang a few phrases and found it easy to fill the auditorium with sound, but of course it is no test of the acoustic qualities of a building to sing in it unless it contains a large audience. It is to be feared that notwithstanding the *soldi* bestowed upon him,

the old *custode* of the place will remember
me with some resentment, for when he told
me the measurements of the auditorium and
"swelled wisibly" with pride, I wickedly
remarked that the Metropolitan Opera
House in New York was larger by several
feet each way. You should have seen how
he glared at me as he replied: " *No, Signore ! non è possibile che c'è un altro teatro
in tutto il mondo grande come La Scala.*"
He was charmingly furious, and I liked him
well for bristling up in defence of the historic structure in his charge.

Any temporary closing of La Scala is of
course a time of harvest for some other
theatre, and so last evening the Teatro dal
Verme was filled to overflowing. The
opera was "Ruy Blas," and the performance of it in all respects excellent, so Milan has given me music for my last days in
Italy.

To-day I have been to one of the operatic agencies in the Galleria to sing for
a well-known *entrepreneur.* He was extremely courteous, and told me there would
be no trouble about getting engagements
for me in the autumn if I chose to return

to Italy. He also gave me a very kind letter of introduction to an agent in Paris.

And here I cease a little from striving and can feel calmly sure that all worthy effort past will yet avail. There is large promise of that in this brilliant, rushing, inspiring spring, wherein all things grow anew out of the darkness and cold that have hidden them away so long. It is good to rest for a time, before going to chillier lands, here in the brightness which gleams on the marbles of the Duomo, a building Mozart-like, grand with a thousand piled-up prettinesses. To-morrow I journey northward.

Printed from American Plates
BALLANTYNE, HANSON & CO.
London & Edinburgh

www.ingramcontent.com/pod-product-compliance
Lightning Source LLC
Chambersburg PA
CBHW020810060726

47498CB00017B/1372